# HOMICIDE
## IN HATTERAS

An Amanda Rittenhouse Mystery #2

# KATE MERRILL

BELLA
BOOKS
2018

Bella Books, Inc.
P.O. Box 10543
Tallahassee, FL 32302

First Bella Books Edition 2018

Editor: Ann Roberts
Cover Designer: Judith Fellows

ISBN: 978-1-59493-591-6

## Other Bella Books by Kate Merrill

### Amanda Rittenhouse Mystery
*Murder at Metrolina*

### Other Books by Kate Merrill

#### Romance
*Northern Lights* (as Christie Cole)
*Flames of Summer*

### Diana Rittenhouse Mystery Series
*A Lethal Listing*
*Blood Brothers*
*Crimes of Commission*
*Dooley Is Dead*
*Buyer Beware*

## Acknowledgments

Thanks to the haunting beauty, mythology, and mystery of North Carolina's Outer Banks, and to Anita and Sandra, the dear friends who introduced us.

Thanks to my wife, Susan, for laughing at all my first drafts and for coaxing me to lose most of the silly stuff.

Thanks to Linda Hill and the wonderfully supportive team at Bella Books for bringing Amanda Rittenhouse to her generous readers.

Special thanks to Ann Roberts, mystery author and editor extraordinaire, who helped me make this a much better book.

She even showed me where I skipped a day.

Gracias and merci beaucoup.

## About the Author

Kate Merrill is an art gallery owner and real estate broker with a lifelong passion for writing. She lives with her spouse, two rescue dogs, and two inherited cats, on Lake Norman in North Carolina. When she is not writing, working with the art community, or selling real estate, she enjoys swimming, boating, and allowing her two strong-headed golden retrievers to take her for a walk.

## Dedication

To Anita, Sandra, Alice, Ranice, Linda, Susan F., Barbara, and my Susan. May our hopefully annual pilgrimages to OBX be filled with food and fun rather than murder and mayhem.

# CHAPTER ONE

*A study in contrasts...*

"You want a heroin addict to bake my sister's wedding cake? Seriously?" Amanda Rittenhouse glanced at Sara Orlando, who was driving.

"Recovering addict. Tammy's been clean two years. She's doing the twelve-step program and attends Narcotics Anonymous right here in Mooresville." Sara sighed and glanced at Amanda with her amazing emerald eyes. "I explained all this before and you were okay with it. You said you wanted to give Tammy a chance."

"Right. I do." Amanda squirmed on the seat. Even with the air-conditioning at full blast, the black leather in Sara's Mazda MX-5 Miata convertible stuck to the backs of her thighs where her shorts ended.

"Well, that's good, then. You'll like Tammy. I promise." Sara reached over with her small hand and squeezed Amanda's knee.

Though her fingers were warm, Sara's touch sent a chill, more like a thrill, straight up Amanda's spine. And she realized it wasn't the prospect of an ex-addict baking the cake that alarmed her, but rather being in such close quarters with Sara. They had met less than three months ago, and the attraction had been immediate and electric. In that short time, they had shared traumatic events, become lovers, and spent as much time together as possible. Yet Amanda barely knew this woman. In fact, this was the first time they had ridden together in a car.

"Relax, Mandy." Sara laughed, a deep-throated sound that always reminded her of the Liberty Bell. "You're just nervous about the wedding. But hey, you volunteered to buy Ginny's cake."

"Yes, I did, and it was a stupid idea. What do I know about cakes?"

"So that's why you need Tammy."

As they drove into the old part of Mooresville and turned right on Main Street, moving into the poorer section of the small town, the brutal sun of a North Carolina July beat down on the convertible top. It made the interior smell like a heated canvas pup tent, time-warping Amanda back to her childhood days at summer camp, when sandwiched into those tents with other giggling girls smelling of Noxzema, she first suspected she was gay.

With her right hand now casually resting on Amanda's thigh, Sara said, "I noticed when you mentioned Ginny you called her your *sister*, not your *stepsister*. Why?"

"Oh, give me a break, Sara. Are you trying to psychoanalyze me again?"

It was true. Dr. Sara Orlando was a shrink. She worked for the city of Charlotte as a counselor, mostly to the homeless and parolees. Tammy Tillman, former prisoner, was one of Sara's favorite clients, thus the recommendation that Tammy become Amanda's chosen baker.

Since Amanda was a metal sculptor, she found Sara's profession exotic, like the two of them perceived life from different sides of the brain. She also knew Sara was selflessly dedicated to her patients and admired her for that. It was only when Sara turned her scalpel-like scrutiny to dissect Amanda's mind that it became decidedly uncomfortable.

"Seriously, I never heard you call Ginny your sister before. It seems like you've both gotten really close."

"Yeah, we're close," she conceded. "What would you expect? We both ran away from home ten years ago, when we were only eighteen, and we've both managed to completely fuck up our lives."

"And you both came through as amazing human beings who share two great parents. So it's all good, right?"

She grunted in the affirmative. Someday she would tell the full story of her and Ginny's dysfunctional families, but it was a long and complex tale. Even she was having trouble accepting her newfound happiness, so she couldn't possibly explain it to Sara, not until they knew one another a whole lot better.

"Make a left after you pass the old mill. According to her address, Tammy lives in mill town." Not a neighborhood where one should park a shiny new red sports car. "Does she run her bakery out of her house?"

"Well, I gather the house actually belonged to an aunt on her father's side. The aunt left it to Tammy in her will."

"Is that even legal? Running a business out of her house?"

"Who knows, who cares? I'm just glad the woman has an entrepreneurial spirit and the desire to make a go of it."

She could easily imagine the Department of Health and Sanitation coming down on Tammy Tillman like a ten-pound hammer.

As Sara removed her hand from Amanda's thigh to slow and downshift, Amanda was both disappointed and relieved by the loss of physical contact.

The street could best be described as "southern seedy." The rows of decrepit wooden bungalows had once been occupied by middle-class factory workers who made blue jeans, but when those jobs moved overseas, the neighborhood decayed slowly. Today, on a steamy summer Sunday, malodorous garbage spilled from cans lining the cracked curbs, awaiting Monday pickup. Junk cars sat on concrete blocks, couches on porches leaked upholstery stuffing, and a group of kids—black and white— played half-naked in a gushing water hydrant that had been forced open at the end of the block. None of this boded well for Ginny's wedding cake.

"Yikes." Even Sara was shocked by the poverty as they parked in front of Tammy's place. "I guess I should lock the car."

"I think you should stay with the car." Amanda nodded at two punks across the street who were greedily eyeing the hubcaps.

"Maybe I'll introduce you guys, then sit out on the porch where I can keep those kids honest."

"Sounds like a plan."

After they climbed out of the Miata, she noticed their elongated shadows creeping across the yard. Hers was tall and skinny, Sara's short and voluptuous. They were a study in contrasts. Amanda was fair, freckled, and prone to sunburn with very short, duck-down blond hair. Sara's Puerto Rican genes gave her flawless, sun-loving skin, silken shoulder-length black hair, full red lips, and hypnotic green eyes. Both were twenty-eight years old.

The old cliché that opposites attract definitely applied. While Amanda was somewhat reserved and shy, Sara was bold and outgoing. The first and only time they had managed to make love, she'd worried about how their vastly different bodies would fit together, but it worked out just fine. More than fine, it was a fireworks spectacular. Since then, they'd been on a high-tension tightrope in anticipation of a repeat performance.

When they stepped onto Tammy's sagging porch, a pit bull in the yard next door began barking viciously and flinging his teeth against the chain-link fence between them.

"Jesus Christ!" Sara jumped.

A woman Amanda presumed was Tammy opened the screen door and screamed, "Aw, shut up, Hamilton!" He stopped barking and slinked off to the far side of his pen. The shaggy dishwater blonde had the figure of a young girl but the eyes of an old lady.

"Hey, y'all. Welcome to my home."

# CHAPTER TWO

*You'll be my date...*

Tammy Tillman's furniture was shabby, but the house, particularly the kitchen, was meticulously clean. This boded well for Ginny's wedding cake.

With Sara keeping a watchful eye on the punks across the street, they moved into the tiny space, which smelled of vanilla and hot baked goods. Amanda's stomach growled when Tammy lifted a large tray of samples from a cupboard that included bite-sized slices of white, yellow, and chocolate iced cake in every conceivable combination from lemon to strawberry.

"So you can taste everything I offer," Tammy explained as she brought an oversized photo album from a drawer. "And these are pictures of all the cakes I've made, all the way up to a six-tiered number I call Royal Wedding."

"Wow!" Sara and Amanda said in unison.

Tammy seemed to sense that Sara was uneasy about her car and suggested they do the taste tests out on the front porch. "It's too damned hot in here anyway. These floor fans can't keep up."

Tammy's hands shook when she passed Amanda a tray holding multicolored metal glasses and a tall, frosted pitcher of iced water. Well, that was fine. Amanda was a bit shaky herself. She had left the hospital only one week ago, and her side still ached from where a bullet had cracked her ribs. She had been shot by a crazed exhibitor at Metrolina Expo, where she had been showing her sculpture and where she first met Sara. The two of them had been instrumental in solving a bizarre murder, not the most auspicious way to begin a love affair. On the bright side, at least the docs had recently removed the splint from the middle finger of Amanda's left hand, which was a relief, because the broken finger had stuck straight up in a perpetual obscene gesture.

"Love the table!" she commented, dragging her mind back to the present as they set the trays on an old wood-paneled door painted turquoise and suspended on four upended concrete blocks.

"Thanks." Tammy offered a quick smile, then glared at the two punks who were now dribbling a basketball in the street, moving closer to Sara's hubcaps. The rhythmic thunk—thunk—thunk made communicating hard. "Hey, you two!" she hollered. "Don't you have something better to do?"

For a wisp of a woman and substantial as a sparrow, Tammy's voice and attitude packed a punch. The teenagers growled a little but then moved down the street to play with the kids at the hydrant. Even Hamilton the pit bull crawled into his doghouse.

"There, now we can hear ourselves think. Have a seat, girls."

They eased onto a cushioned glider, while Tammy played hostess, handing them each a pile of napkins. "Don't be shy, now, dig in."

Amanda needed no coaxing as she greedily sampled the cakes. Neither did Sara. Soon both were making un-ladylike guttural sounds of approval. A tiny smear of strawberry icing clung to Sara's upper lip. She longed to lick it away. In the meantime, Tammy looked on with motherly satisfaction, which was odd, since Amanda knew Tammy was only twenty-two, more like a little sister. Yet the weary look in her strange pale blue eyes betrayed the rough life she had endured so far.

"Now, tell me something about the bride and groom," Tammy said. "Maybe it'll help us decide how to style the cake."

Amanda wiped her lips and described the tumultuous romance between her stepsister, Ginny Troutman, and Ginny's high school lover, Trevor Dula. She explained how Ginny had run away from North Carolina to Galveston when her mother died. As soon as she settled in Texas, she realized she was pregnant and married an abusive oil man, old enough to be her daddy. Seven months later she gave birth to her daughter, Lissa. Finally Ginny divorced the oil man, got a job as a croupier in Las Vegas, and eventually returned home when her father, Matthew Troutman, married Diana Rittenhouse, Amanda's mother.

"Wow, that's quite a story!" Tammy exclaimed. "So let me guess. Now Ginny is reunited with Trev, the love of her life, and little Lissa has herself a *real* daddy, isn't that right?" Tammy grinned. "Well, at least we've got us a happy ending. I'd say that calls for something special on top of this cake." With that, she scuttled back inside the house, leaving Amanda and Sara on the glider.

"Is that a true story?" Sara asked.

"Oh, yeah, but it's not the whole story. I left out all the gory details about the murder that brought them together." The saga of Ginny and Trev was yet another little piece of Amanda's life she'd not yet shared with Sara. "I'll tell you all about it when we have more time."

"It sounds like we need another sleepover," Sara whispered suggestively as she took her hand. "It's ironic that a murder brought us together too."

She laughed. "Ironic indeed. Up until this year, I would have said my mother was the crime magnet, but now I'm not so sure."

But truthfully, the past three months since her homecoming had shaken her to the core. Reuniting with her estranged mom, Diana, and gaining a nurturing extended family had been an unexpected blessing. Meeting Sara, after giving up on love, was beyond amazing. Almost losing her life to a crazed killer—that she could have done without.

Sara squeezed her hand. "Yes, you've told me about Diana's adventures as an amateur sleuth. Like I said, scary stories are great for a slumber party."

A blush crept up Amanda's neck. When Sara used her seductive voice, it sent a surge of heat to all the right places. It also made her shy, so she slipped away from her hand. Yet she loved how the hot summer afternoon moistened the skin on Sara's forehead and upper lip, and the way the shadows shifted on her bare shoulders. Amanda needed a hug and a kiss badly, but she had no desire to put on a show for the neighborhood.

Luckily they were interrupted by Tammy, who pushed through the screen door carrying a large cardboard box covered with gold silk. "These are the toppers." She set the box on the floor between them and removed miniature plastic figurines of brides and grooms of all races, clad in many different fashions. She had tiny wedding bells, musical instruments, gazebos, and lovebirds. "Now, ladies, choose something that suits Ginny and Trevor."

"A marriage toy box," Amanda muttered. Without hesitation she picked a bride in a miniskirt with a little pink guitar, and a groom who was a cross between Elvis and GI Joe. "These are perfect! I can't believe you had a guitar to go with this sassy bride."

"Really? Are you sure?" Tammy must have expected something more traditional.

"Absolutely." Amanda made the statues do a happy dance.

"What about this?" Sara picked up two brides—one a tall, skinny blonde, the other short and dark. "Did you ever bake a cake for two women?"

Tammy's eyes expanded like transparent blue marbles. "Oh, no, I never did one of *those* weddings!"

"Would that be a problem for you, Tammy?"

Amanda was shocked. Yes, Sara was Tammy's therapist, but how much had she shared about her private life? Resisting an urge to hide under the turquoise table, Amanda held her breath and waited for the awkward moment to pass.

Finally Tammy began to giggle. The sound started deep in her throat and bubbled up through her lips. "You think I'm one of those ignorant, redneck gay-bashers? The ones who beat their Bibles and pretend they're not bigots? Hell no, Doc. You know me better than that. You find some same-sex couples who want to get hitched and send them my way. It would be an honor."

Sara smiled and high-fived her patient, and Amanda exhaled in relief. They concluded their business quickly. Amanda chose a three-tiered cake in three flavors, iced in white frosting. She wrote a check, gave Tammy the pertinent time and directions to the house where the wedding would be held, and they said their goodbyes.

"You almost gave me a heart attack in there, Sara!"

"Calm down, darlin'." She smiled and winked. "I knew Tammy would be cool with the idea of a gay wedding. After all, I've been inside her head quite a lot lately."

"Even so..." Amanda wasn't about to let her off the hook that easily. Sara knew she was only halfway out of the closet and easily embarrassed. "I think you take malicious delight in teasing me."

"I think you're afraid to acknowledge me in public."

She thought about it, noting the catch in Sara's voice, and recognized a grain of truth. "You're wrong," she said at last.

"Prove it."

She took her hand without even checking to see if someone was watching. "Okay, come with me to Ginny's wedding. You'll be my date."

# CHAPTER THREE

*Playing dress-up…*

The Saturday of Ginny's wedding could not have been more perfect. The guests arrived and parked along the dead-end street leading to Mom and Matthew's house on Lake Norman. The mood was relaxed and upbeat as those in attendance greeted their hosts, then strolled down the freshly mown lawn to water's edge. Rows of chairs faced the gazebo where the service would be held.

The sky was robin's-egg blue with a trace of thready clouds high above and a gentle breeze to blow away the heat and the humidity. Uninvited guests in sailboats and motorboats steered close to the shore, bobbing on the waves, curious to see what all the fuss was about.

"They're like gawkers at a traffic accident," Amanda complained.

"This wedding is no traffic accident," her mother objected. "I'm sure our yard looks pretty from the lake, and those boaters just want a little piece of the romance."

In her role as maid of honor, Amanda was obliged to wear a silly pastel blue sheath dress that skimmed the tops of her knees in front, then dipped down to midcalf like a faux train in back. The outfit included a fringed scarf in bright abstract tones of green, tangerine, and hot pink. It hung loosely around her neck and flapped around in front. As matron of honor, her mother wore a pale green dress like Amanda's and the same dumb scarf. Ginny's seven-year-old daughter, Lissa, the flower girl, got a pale pink dress and a little version of the scarf tied like a flopping bow in her flaming-red hair.

"These high heels are killing me," she grumbled as she accepted a glass of white wine and a warm cheese puff from a boy carrying a silver tray. "And where did Ginny find these waiters? They look like high school kids."

"That's because they are high school kids. Matthew drafted them from that automotive class he teaches once a week."

"I thought I saw grease under that boy's fingernails."

"For heaven's sake, knock it off, Mandy. I know you hate playing dress-up, but you'll be able to lose the heels soon," Mom finished with a grimace.

Now that made Amanda smile. Ginny's instructions specified that those in the wedding party must kick off their shoes and walk barefoot down the grassy aisle. This included the bride and the groom and was supposed to symbolize comfort and freedom in their marriage. Mom absolutely hated the idea.

"Is your friend Sara here yet? I'm eager to meet her."

"Not yet." She'd been anxiously watching for a red Miata and was worried because Tammy was late. The plan was to serve the cake right after the service, then most of the guests would leave. Close friends and family, including Sara, would then drive up to Buffalo Guys, the nightclub Trev owned. There they would be treated to dinner.

Excusing herself, Amanda wandered back to the road to watch the incoming traffic. By the time she reached the driveway, a battered gray Toyota pulled in and parked. Tammy Tillman leaped from the passenger seat. Her straggly blond hair was subdued in a ponytail and she wore a crisp white shirt, black trousers and bow tie.

"Jeez, I'm sorry I'm late," she said. "But the cake's in the back and it's awesome."

Before she could respond, a surly looking man climbed from the passenger's side and glared at her. He was tall and muscle-bound, with a blond crew cut and bloodshot blue eyes. Amanda figured he was too old to be Tammy's boyfriend and too young to be her daddy. Either way, he looked like a cage wrestler with his tattoos, black wife-beater T-shirt, and tight jeans. She sincerely hoped he wasn't Tammy's assistant and wouldn't have contact with their guests.

"This here is Sonny Roach," Tammy explained. "He's my mom's boyfriend, visiting from the beach. He'll help me bring in the cake, but then he's gonna wait in the car."

"Hi, Sonny." Amanda did not hold out her hand for him to shake, which was a good thing, because the man barely acknowledged the introduction. Instead, he pivoted in his alligator boots and stomped to the back of the car.

"Don't mind him. He's a jerk," Tammy said quickly.

She was nervous, talking so fast Amanda wondered if she was on speed. Like Sonny, her eyes were bloodshot, but more like she'd been crying, not using drugs.

"Are you okay, Tammy? Can I help?"

"No, Mandy, I'm good. Just point me to the kitchen and everything will be ready when you are."

By the time she'd set them up in the kitchen and Sonny had retreated to the Toyota as promised, Amanda stepped outside and nearly collided with Sara. The woman took her breath away. She wore a soft, emerald green pantsuit that brought out her eyes and a low-cut cream silk shell that showed off her cleavage. A single strand of pearls glowed against her deeply tanned throat as she gave Amanda a wicked smile.

"Hey, babe," Sara said. "You look like an honorable maid."

"Thanks. You clean up pretty good too, Doc."

Her heart fluttered as she led Sara down to the first row, bride's side. Along the way, she snagged a high school kid and supplied Sara with wine and a dainty plate of canapes. The seat next to Sara's had been reserved for Amanda so they could sit together after she completed her part in the ceremony.

"Mandy, do you remember that first day I saw you when you were in the hospital?"

"Yes, it was the day the Supreme Court decided *Obergefell v. Hodges*, entitling same-sex couples to marry nationwide."

"Good memory. So maybe someday we will attend one of *those* weddings?"

"Maybe so." But she could not imagine such a thing. At the same moment, she heard the dinner bell ringing up at the house, the signal that the service was about to begin. "Looks like I'm on. Wish me luck."

# CHAPTER FOUR

*I do…*

The next half hour passed in a blur, like a film sequence in slow motion. Amanda recalled the audience laughing and clapping when she and mom kicked off their heels and led the procession. During that long walk toward the gazebo, a mated pair of white-tailed hawks soared drunkenly in the sky and a hush fell on the boaters out on the lake. From the corner of her eye, she saw Sara watching from the first row, a radiant smile on her face.

Soon after they turned to watch for the bride, Trev Dula and his disreputable Uncle Maynard walked up from the side, both barefoot. Trev was as tall, dark, and handsome as usual in a cream suit, electric-blue dress shirt, and tie in the scarf colors. Maynard had washed and ponytailed his unruly gray hair, while his long-sleeved tangerine shirt and obligatory scarf mostly hid his tattoos. Both stood at attention beside Mom, Amanda, and the Troutman family minister, who looked out of place in his conservative dark suit.

As they awaited the bride, Amanda touched the groom's hand.

"Are you okay, Trev?"

He nodded, a brave smile on his lips and a mist of tears in his eyes. This display of emotion from the ultra-tough combat marine brought a painful lump to her throat. She almost lost it when the guitarist played an electric riff of the "Wedding March." When Lissa skipped toward them, tossing flowers at the guests and Ginny appeared on Trout's arm, the lump in Amanda's throat thickened.

Trout, as everyone called Matthew Troutman, was calm and solemn as he led his daughter to the altar, but Ginny was outrageous in her extreme version of *the dress*. Employing all the colors in psychedelic intensity, it was a miniskirt in front, an exaggerated train behind, and her bare toenails were painted hot pink.

Everyone stood and clapped as she sashayed toward Trev. When she arrived, she winked at Amanda, then took Trev's hand. When he gulped with emotion, Amanda really lost it.

Luckily this was her cue to be seated. She barely made it to her chair before the sobs came. She choked them back as much as possible as Sara handed her a tissue.

"Whoa, I didn't expect you to be a romantic," Sara whispered in her ear. "Do you always cry at weddings?"

"I do."

# CHAPTER FIVE

*The coward's way out...*

Possibly Amanda would have made it through the day without incident had it not been for the cake ceremony. She had managed to get her emotions under control until Ginny was properly hitched, but then she and Sara joined the others up on the deck where the champagne flowed freely.

"Where did all these people come from?" Sara wondered. "Ginny's only been back in North Carolina a few months. Does she still have so many friends from her distant past?"

"Not really. Most of the young people are Trev's buddies, vets and their wives, and the older folks are friends of Mom and Trout."

"Motley-looking crew," Sara commented. "But they sure know how to have fun."

"Yes, we do!" Mom came up behind them in line. She gave Amanda a kiss on the cheek and beamed at Sara. "Hi, I'm Mandy's mom, in case you haven't guessed."

"You sure you're not her sister?" Sara grinned and gave her a hug as both mother and daughter groaned. "Yeah, I bet you get that a lot. But really, you look so much alike."

It was true. They were both tall and lanky with the same short blond hair and intense blue eyes. When they were first reunited, Amanda had resented the constant comparisons, but now she liked them. Mom's hair was now mostly white and she had laugh lines at her mouth and eyes, but other than that, they could be mistaken as twins at a distance.

"Mandy, do you remember Trev's friend, Charles Hinson?" Her mom grabbed a man waiting in line behind them and pulled him forward.

"Sure, I do. Hi, Chip!" She shook his big hand. She'd met him several times at Buffalo Guys and knew he was Trev's business partner and best friend. "Can you believe Trev's actually tied the knot?"

"He's loved Ginny forever, but she's way too good for him."

Chip Hinson had the sharp good looks of a *Vogue* model and the body of a weightlifter. It was hard to believe he was actually a mild-mannered accountant. He took the arm of a tall African American man standing nearby and drew him forward. "This is my boyfriend, Rodney Green. We've been together three years now and we're thinking about getting married."

Amanda felt her mom stiffen and could not believe her ears. She knew Chip was gay, but her mom did not. If only she could disappear in a puff of fairy dust, she would do so. Why did he have to be so damned open about his sexuality? It made it difficult for everyone, especially her.

Sara reacted first. "Congratulations, guys!" She gave each man a little hug and looked expectantly at Amanda.

She could either strike out, or hit a homer. It was time to introduce Sara, and she had two choices: come clean about their relationship or stay in the closet. She realized in that instant that she owed everyone the truth, especially Sara. She also understood that her mother was an open-minded liberal who would surely embrace her lifestyle, but she and her mother had never had *the talk*. Their relationship was still fragile. So in the end, she took the coward's way out, mumbling good wishes to the men and introducing her as a friend.

Everyone was cool with it, but she sensed Sara shrinking into herself, a look of disappointment on her face.

As soon as they were alone, Sara grabbed her arm. "What's with you, Mandy? I thought I was supposed to be your date."

"Well, you are my date."

"Doesn't feel that way."

To make matters worse, Mom appeared with yet another single man on her arm. "Sara, meet Dr. Joe Silverman. Joe is a psychiatrist at the VA Hospital, where he and Trevor became friends. I expect you two will have a lot in common."

She practically pushed them into one another's arms. She had always loved to play Cupid. Even when Amanda was in high school, her mother had coaxed her to date a young Harvard-bound quarterback on the football team, when all she wanted was to hang out with the girls in the cheering block.

She had only herself to blame when Sara left with Joe Silverman. Sara glanced back only once at her.

"Shit!" she muttered just before Chip and Rodney captured both her arms.

"Cheer up, girl," Chip said. "Someday it'll be your turn at the altar."

"Right. Your friend Sara is a good-looking woman. Do you two have a thing going?" Rodney asked, a mischievous glint in his dark eyes.

"Shut up, you two. Don't you want to sample the wedding cake?" Hell, did everyone know but her mother? Ginny knew the score, had even met Amanda's ex in Sarasota, Florida. But had she blabbed to everyone at Buffalo Guys? "The woman who baked the cake is looking for gay customers, so you two should meet her."

"Why not?" Chip agreed as he elbowed Rodney's ribs.

Sure enough, the cake was as awesome as Tammy had promised. The crowd had already made a dent in the three layers. Amanda was relieved that after Ginny and Trev took their first bites, they fed it to one another gently, rather than smashing it into one another's mouths, as was the disgusting custom.

"Look, Mommy gave me the little pink guitar from on top of the cake!" Suddenly Lissa was at their knees, jumping up and down on a sugar high.

"Very cool," Rodney said. "Where are your parents going for their honeymoon, Disney World?"

Lissa was confused. "That's for kids. They're going to Paris."

"No kidding?" Rodney seemed appropriately impressed, like the family had been when the couple announced their plans. But Amanda was not looking forward to the next two weeks when, as the only resident adult not gainfully employed, she would become babysitter-in-chief.

The cake tasted as yummy as it looked, but when she introduced Chip and Rodney to Tammy, the baker seemed oddly distracted, kept glancing over her shoulder as she served up the slices. She also snapped impatiently when the guys asked her to email them a price list.

"Are you all right?" Amanda whispered to her in a private moment.

"Not really. I should never have let that asshole come along."

Amanda assumed she meant Sonny. "What's the problem?" Looking around, she spotted him lounging against the Toyota, glaring in Tammy's direction.

"He said he wanted to help, but that's bullshit."

"No kidding?"

Obviously Sonny had an agenda, which seemed to include disrupting the party as he strode toward the deck.

"Listen, Tammy, can you please keep him out of the way?" she begged. "Maybe he can wait in the kitchen?"

"He can wait in hell, for all I care."

Clearly the situation was escalating, and Amanda desperately wanted to head off any trouble. She excused herself, took Tammy's arm and guided her around to the backyard, behind the house, out of sight.

Sonny Roach followed.

"Don't walk away from me, bitch!" he hollered, suddenly upon them. "I asked you before. Where did you hide my money?"

"Go fuck yourself!" Tammy jabbed her middle finger into his face.

Amanda inserted herself between them just in time to block the punch Sonny leveled at Tammy. Unfortunately she blocked it with her jaw. The sudden stunning impact brought tears to her eyes. She did not see stars, but she did see red and wanted to pulverize him.

Before she could fight back, Tammy started howling and beating his chest with her fists. They were like little pistons hammering him backward, but only for a moment. As Amanda watched in horror, he boxed two solid punches to Tammy's stomach, and when she was doubled over, he finished with a slap to her face, making her wilt into his arms.

Amanda didn't realize she was screaming until Chip and Rodney rounded the house and began shouting at Sonny. The sight of the two big men startled him, but did not slow his enraged momentum. He was about to hit Tammy again when Rodney pinned his arms and dragged him backward, allowing her to escape.

"Someone call the cops!" Chip yelled.

"Stay out of this, man," Sonny roared. "This is family business, you hear?"

Tammy took the opportunity to deliver a vicious kick to Sonny's groin, leaving him squealing in pain. She made a beeline to her car, flung herself inside, and started the engine. Before anyone could react, the Toyota peeled out and sped down the street.

"Jesus Christ, what just happened?" Rodney let go of Sonny's arms and grimaced as Sonny cradled his crotch. "Should we call 911?"

Sara joined the upset trio. She watched in horror as Sonny shouted obscenities and staggered toward the road. Her normally tanned skin was deathly pale, and her lips formed a perfect "O" as she beheld Amanda's face. "Ooh, baby, you're gonna have one helluva bruise. Did Tammy's friend do this to you?"

She nodded in misery. "But I'm pretty sure that jerk is not Tammy's friend. Please, let's not call the police. It will spoil the wedding."

Sara crossed her arms and considered. "It would also be disastrous for Tammy's parole status."

"What about him?" Chip pointed at Sonny, who had limped his way to the corner. "Should we offer him a ride or something?"

"No way," Rodney scoffed. "That asshole can take care of himself. Let him hitch."

"What about Tammy? Do you think she's all right?" Amanda worried. "Sara, you should call her in an hour or so to make sure she got home safe."

"Should I?" Sara had a curious look on her face.

"Tammy left all her plates behind." Even as she said it, she knew it was a stupid remark. "Are you still coming to the dinner at Buffalo Guys tonight, Sara?"

She touched Amanda's cheek. "Maybe you should consider staying home. You took a nasty punch."

"No, we should still go!" Amanda exclaimed defiantly. She needed some quality time alone with Sara to make amends.

But Sara stepped back a few paces and pinched the bridge of her nose, like she was warding off a massive headache. "You know what, Mandy? If you insist on going, then go alone. I have a *real* date with Joe Silverman."

# CHAPTER SIX

*Growing a backbone...*

The after-party at Buffalo Guys was a huge success—beer flowing, music blaring, and the main event: Ginny and Trev, along with Chip and Rodney, performing an X-rated tango on the dance floor. Everyone had fun except Amanda, whose sick headache throbbed in time with the bass woofer and drove her to the relative quiet of the deck. She couldn't stop thinking about Sara and Joe Silverman. She knew damn well Sara was one hundred percent lesbian, not bi. She had only accepted the date to spite her, but that didn't make it any less hurtful. Finally, as she stared unseeing into the lake, she got an update from Sara.

"I called Tammy and she's okay."

"Are you sure? What about Sonny Roach?"

"I don't know, but Tammy said everything was cool." Sara's voice was beyond cool. It was dry ice. "I hear from the background music that you decided to attend the party."

"Yes, I did. Are you having a fun date with Joe Silverman?"

Silence. "Look, I'll call you Monday. Why don't you go home now and get some rest?"

And she did. Amanda left early with her mother and Trout, and Sunday she slept the sleep of the dead. Fortunately the bruise did not show its true colors—marbleized purple and yellow—until Monday morning. This allowed her to conceal the unpleasant incident until Ginny and Trev had flown away to the City of Lights.

By Monday afternoon, having lied to her hovering mother about the injury, saying she had walked into a door, she now found herself sitting cross-legged on the floor of Trout's abandoned garage. She was soul-searching, wondering not what the hell she would do with the rest of her life, but rather what she should do with her immediate future.

The garage, located at her stepfather's place of business, offered one path, because Trout said she could have it rent-free as a welding studio. The advantage was it was close to home, that is, close to Mom and Trout's house, where she'd been living since she returned to North Carolina. But as much as she loved them, the situation was not ideal because she hated being the cliché of a rootless adult child living off her parents.

Soon she'd have enough money to strike out on her own, thanks to a big commission she'd received from Wells Fargo. The bank had hired her to create a large steel abstract for a new branch office, and she could live off the proceeds for at least two years.

She'd won the job while showing her art at Metrolina Expo in Charlotte, where she'd been shot by that murderous exhibitor. The injuries she'd sustained prevented her from beginning the heavy work of manhandling and welding large sheets of steel, but Wells Fargo had been understanding and extended their deadline. She expected to be fit enough to begin work in August.

Should she keep her studio space at Metrolina, or let it go in favor of Trout's garage? Metrolina conjured up bad memories, but the garage promoted more dependency on her parents. The Charlotte location anchored her closer to Sara, but the way things had been going between them lately…

*Shit!* She climbed stiffly to her feet. She was angry at the persistent pain in her side, fed up with her stiff finger, but mostly she was tired of being a wimp hiding in the closet.

"Grow a backbone!" she shouted at the empty space. Her outburst startled a dumpy little Carolina wren perched on the windowsill. It flew into a nearby poplar and gave her a dirty look.

At the same time, her cell phone vibrated in the pocket of her jeans.

"What?"

"Well, hello to you too," Sara responded.

Her anger dissolved to shame. After all, Sara's was the one voice she wanted to hear. "Sorry, you caught me at a bad time."

"I know what you mean. I'm having a bad time too."

"What's wrong?"

"I'm not sure…" She sighed. "I have a regular weekly session scheduled with Tammy, but she didn't show up today. That's never happened before, so I'm really worried. It's a condition of her parole, so she takes it very seriously. Now I'm afraid it has something to do with that Neanderthal who punched you."

Amanda feared the same thing. "Maybe we should have called the police?"

"Hindsight is always twenty-twenty, and I guess we share the blame on this one. But I don't get it. When I called her Saturday night, Tammy said she was fine."

"Yes, but should we have believed her?"

Sara was silent a moment. "We should have double-checked somehow, but I was too busy licking my personal wounds to care much about anyone else. I'm sorry about the way I behaved. I acted like a jealous schoolgirl. Please forgive me."

She swallowed the lump in her throat. "No, forgive *me*. Next time I'll do better."

More silence. "Let's just forget it and start over. The important thing now is Tammy. I've been phoning her nonstop, but her voice mailbox is full. I've texted her, but no response."

"What can we do?"

Beyond the garage window the birds kept singing and shadows lengthened across River Highway as the first commuters returned with the evening rush hour.

"Could you do me an enormous favor, Mandy?"

"Name it."

"You're so close, would you drive over to Tammy's house to check on her?"

She recalled the pit bull and the punks with the basketball. The idea was not appealing, but she felt deeply responsible. "No problem. I have the perfect excuse. Mom and I washed and boxed Tammy's plates this morning. I'll load them in my van and return them."

"Oh, that would be a huge relief. But maybe you should ask Diana or Trout to ride along?"

"Right." She pretended to agree, but she had already decided self-sufficiency was part of her new growing-a-backbone program. "I'll go right away and call you when I have some news."

Sara took a deep breath. "Thanks so much, babe. And I have something else to confess…"

"I never did go out with Joe Silverman."

# CHAPTER SEVEN

*Really bad trouble...*

Amanda figured Moby Dyke, her big white work van, would not inspire hubcap thieves, even in mill town, although one of the punks from across the street eyed her as she struggled up Tammy's front steps with the heavy load of dishes. At least Hamilton the pit bull was polite this time. He must have remembered her from before, because he only growled gently and did not leave his house while she rang the doorbell.

"Anybody home?" She had not seen Tammy's Toyota on the block, but possibly it was parked back in the alley. She definitely hoped Sonny was not in the house. The last thing she wanted was another confrontation, but maybe the thug would notice her ugly bruise, be overcome by guilt, and leave her the hell alone.

"Tammy?" she called. "It's Amanda Rittenhouse. I'm returning your dishes."

When she got no response, she set the box on the turquoise table and rapped hard on the door. Much to her surprise, it was unlocked and swung inward to the open house.

"Tammy?" Her voice quavered, and in spite of the heat, goose bumps popped on her arms. She'd watched her share of horror movies, so she knew this was the moment to cut and run. She still had time to escape the maniac lurking in a closet with a knife or avoid tripping over the dead body drenched in blood, but then she heard music playing down the hall in the kitchen.

Of course, that explained it! Tammy was busy baking and the loud music had kept her from hearing the doorbell. She drew a shaky breath and moved toward the kitchen, fully expecting someone to jump out and attack her from behind. Her footsteps echoed, her heartbeats pounded through the silence, and by the time she reached the radio propped in the dish drainer, she knew she had entered an empty house. It felt more than deserted, like the eerie mask of death on a person's face—when the features are peaceful, but the breath of life has departed.

Jesus, she *had* been watching too many horror movies!

She barked out a disgusted laugh at her foolishness, and just for fun, she twisted the knob on the back door. It was locked. Maybe Tammy had left by the alley and simply forgot to lock the front door?

Impulsively she dialed Sara and explained the situation.

"That's strange. Does it look like Tammy left in a hurry?"

"I guess so. She left the radio on." She scanned the kitchen. "And there are dirty dishes in the sink, even a bowl crusted with white icing like the one on Ginny's cake." She walked back into the living room. "God, it's a mess in here. Someone pulled the cushions off the couch, tossed the books off the bookcases, and emptied all the stuff from the sideboard. Even the paintings are crooked. That's not like Tammy. The house was so neat when we were here before."

"Sounds like someone's trashed the place. Have you checked her bedroom?"

She heard the mounting fear in Sara's voice and it spooked her. Yet she automatically moved toward the room where she assumed Tammy slept. The violation of the bedroom was far worse than what she'd witnessed in the main rooms. She gasped when she saw Tammy's stockings, panties, and bras strewn about the floor. All the dresser drawers were pulled out in a tumble and her jewelry lay about in a tangle. The mattress and box spring were shredded, so that bits of foam rubber dusted the room like snow.

"Are you okay, babe? Tell me what you see!"

But Amanda could not utter a word.

"For heaven's sake, Mandy, check out the closet. Are clothes missing? Use your mom's sleuthing genes."

"Oh my God, it's awful! Either someone really hates her guts, or he's intent on scaring her to death." She moved on to the closet. "I see suitcases, but all her clothes have been yanked off the hangers. If Tammy left on a trip, she didn't pack much."

"He's looking for something. Search inside her shoes."

"Are you kidding me? If I get caught, they'll throw me in jail."

Amanda's pulse raced and her fingers trembled as she peeked into Tammy's dirty sneakers, high heels, and boots. She decided she did not need Sara's permission to flee the scene. At the same time, she heard the heavy thud of footsteps coming down the hall in her direction. "Someone's here, Sara! What the hell should I do?"

"Oh shit! Hide yourself, Mandy. Hurry!"

Clearly Sara was panicking, and so was she. She couldn't crawl under the torn-apart bed. She was calculating whether she could squeeze into the littered closet, when the neighborhood punk strode into the bedroom.

"What you doin' in Miss Tammy's house?" he growled.

Though he was only a teenager, the kid outweighed her by fifty pounds. His muscular arms were folded across his chest, and his shorts hung so low they threatened to fall off his hips. The snarl on his purple lips was midway between a smile and a smirk.

"I was returning some dishes Tammy left at my place," she croaked in a squeaky little voice.

"Is that what's in the box you left on the porch?"

He was coherent enough, yet she was still scared witless, mindful of the damage he could inflict. "Yes, the box was too heavy for me. Maybe you could help me carry it in?"

"How much is it worth to you?" He shifted foot to foot, and his oversize athletic shoes made the old floorboards creak.

"Sorry, I don't have any money with me."

"Well, Tammy ain't here anyway," he said as he looked at the devastation. "What the fuck happened here?"

She ignored the question. "Did Tammy go on vacation?"

He giggled. "Not hardly. If she was goin' on vacation, she sure left in a hurry. She come home late yesterday and took off like the devil was on her tail."

Sara shouted something through the phone but she ignored it. "Did Tammy seem scared or upset?"

"She seemed rich." The kid smirked.

"What do you mean?"

"Miss Tammy took a wad of cash outta her bag. Enough money to take her round the world."

Suddenly she remembered how Sonny had accused Tammy of hiding his money, right before he slugged her. "Why would she show you her cash?"

He grinned. "She paid me to keep my mouth shut, and that's exactly what I'm doin'."

Her fear was fast being replaced by annoyance. "Okay, did you happen to see a big man with tattoos with Tammy?"

"What's it worth to you, lady?"

Now she was ready to smack the punk. "I already told you. I don't have any money."

The kid threw back his head and laughed. "I'm just messin' with you. I seen that dude come about an hour after Miss Tammy split."

"Was his name Sonny?"

"I call him fuckhead. He had left his stupid tow truck parked so's no one could get into my driveway. He's the shit who trashed this place."

In spite of his attitude, she sensed the kid was worried about Tammy. "Did you consider calling the police?"

He rolled his eyes, making it clear he thought she was deranged. Folks from mill town did not call cops.

"I guess I could help with that box, though," he added.

Before she could react, he'd retrieved the dishes from the front porch, slid the box on the kitchen table and left.

"Might wanna lock the front door when you go, lady," he hollered over his shoulder.

"What the hell just happened?" Sara was frantic when she retrieved the phone.

"You probably heard, didn't you?"

"Tammy took off, then Sonny came and tore up the place." Sara filled in the blanks. "Are you okay?"

"I think so." But her knees wobbled as she crossed the room and collapsed onto Tammy's displaced mattress.

"So you think Tammy's in trouble?"

She ran her arm under one of Tammy's mutilated pillows and touched something cold, small, and square. She withdrew an abandoned cell phone, the one item no woman would ever willingly leave behind.

"Yes, Sara," she answered slowly. "I'd say Tammy is in really bad trouble."

# CHAPTER EIGHT

*Come with us...*

They met for lunch in Cornelius, the midway point between Amanda's home in Mooresville and Sara's place in Charlotte. The restaurant, Athena's, served both the faithful locals and interstate travelers from the expressway—anyone who loved Greek food.

The table Sara had chosen was under a mural of the *Catawba Queen*, the big-wheel riverboat that cruised Lake Norman. The heavily tinted windows made it feel like evening, in spite of the bright sun outside. The extreme air-conditioning caused Amanda to pull her jacket back on.

"Don't do that," Sara whispered. "I love seeing your freckled shoulders."

She shivered. "Too bad. Eat your grape leaves."

The date was impromptu and unprecedented in the middle of Sara's busy work week, but they had decided to rendezvous because they were worried about Tammy, or at least that was the excuse. Fact was, they simply wanted to be together. Ever since the argument at Ginny's wedding, they needed to reconnect and rekindle that spark.

Actually the fire was already burning just fine, Amanda thought. Sara looked sexy in a sleeveless white silk blouse. Her tanned, freckle-free arms were shapely and smooth, her breasts full and graceful under the soft fabric. The flickering candle in its red glass globe made her long, black hair shine.

"What?" Sara demanded.

"Was I staring? You are beautiful, Sara."

"So are you, babe. I've missed you."

She felt the pressure of Sara's knee under the table and pointedly shucked off her jacket. Buttering a corn stick, she got serious. After the incident, Amanda had called the Mooresville police, without regard as to how the call might negatively impact Tammy's parole status. "But when I followed up, the cops didn't seem particularly concerned about Tammy. They sent a patrol car to her house and interviewed the kid, but it seems Tammy got her money's worth. The little shakedown artist wasn't talking. My guess is they'll write it up as a domestic squabble and won't pursue it."

"Did you tell them about the money?"

She stared at her lap and fiddled with her napkin. "I did try, but they asked me if I'd actually seen any money. Since I never laid eyes on the damned cash, and the kid denied it, I suppose the cops will consider the issue hearsay."

Sara raised her eyebrows. "Maybe not."

"But what if Sonny follows Tammy to get the cash and gets violent? Wouldn't that put her in a terribly dangerous situation?"

Sara nodded slowly. "Absolutely, but it's not your job to do the cops' work for them. I had pretty much the same experience with the Charlotte police when I informed them of this situation." She paused to eat a bite of moussaka. "Mostly they see Tammy's disappearance as a parole violation and they're pissed. Likely they'll try to toss her back in jail when she resurfaces, especially if her urine test comes back positive for drugs."

Amanda carefully removed the bits of onion from her gyro and spread the tzatziki sauce on the ground lamb and pita bread. "Should we have involved the police at all?"

"Sure, then if anything bad happens, we can tell the idiots, 'I told you so.'"

She knew Sara had a love-hate relationship with the officers who sent disturbed clients to her office. In some cases, she sensed Sara identified too closely with her patients, but that caring nature was one of the many things she loved about her. It was also the reason she had to confess.

"I need to tell you something else, Sara." Amanda mustered the courage. "I didn't tell the Mooresville police about Tammy's cell phone. Thing is, I took it."

"You stole her cell phone? Good God, what were you thinking?"

"I thought it might provide a clue and help us find her."

"Well, did it?"

She sighed. "I don't know yet. The phone was completely dead. I'm charging it now."

Sara didn't seem to be able to decide whether to be angry or proud. Finally, she cleared her throat. "I don't know what to say, but please tell me immediately if you get something. In the meantime, I think Tammy might be at the beach. Her good-for-nothing mother lives in Hatteras, and she grew up there. If that slimeball Sonny is really her mother's boyfriend, it's likely they headed for the coast."

All this was news to her. "Did you call Tammy's mother?"

Sara leaned forward, a conspiratorial glint in her exotic green eyes. "Matter of fact, I had Lynette Tillman's number in Tammy's file, so I did call the bitch. She hung up on me right after saying she hadn't seen her worthless daughter in two years."

"Did you believe her?"

"No, I did not believe her. After all my sessions with Tammy, I've learned one true thing: if her mama is talking, she's lying."

"So what do we do about it?"

Sara grinned, allowing a pregnant pause to expand until the coffee came, and she'd deliberately stirred in milk and sweetener. "I do have a plan, and it could include you."

Her palms began to sweat while she waited for an explanation. In the short months she'd known Sara, she'd learned one true thing: when the lovely Puerto Rican shrink got that mischievous look in her eye, it meant trouble.

"Well, spit it out!" she demanded when she could no longer stand the tension.

Sara laughed. "Well, every year I take a vacation to the Outer Banks. We always go with two women we call The Cat Couple. We usually go in October when the beach is less crowded, but the girls tell me they're not opposed to trying a July vacation." She sipped her coffee. "So we've decided to go this coming weekend and stay seven days. I told them about you, and we'd like you to come with us."

Amanda was speechless. Also she was both terrified and excited to meet some other couple as Sara's girlfriend. "Don't you have too much work at the clinic? Can you just up and leave like that?"

She shrugged. "No problem. Summer is my quiet season. Even my patients take vacations. What about you? Can you get away?"

She could think of several excuses to avoid doing this thing she wanted so much. But in fact, Mom and Trout could look after Lissa without her help, and she was physically unfit to begin work on the commissioned sculpture.

She met Sara's intense gaze. "I guess I can go."

"Do you *want* to go? We will be sharing a room—and a bed."

She felt the heat and knew she was blushing tomato red. "You know I do."

Sara's big smile lit up the dark room. "I'm so happy, but there is one thing you should know."

She waited.

"When I said *we* used to go, I meant I used to go with my ex, a woman named Judith Dillinger. The Cat Couple, Jude, and I have been friends forever, so I hope it won't be awkward for you."

# CHAPTER NINE

*Odd woman out...*

Amanda was terrified to meet The Cat Couple, and not just because she'd always been a dog person. Every lesbian who'd been round the block a time or two understood the tight bond couples sometimes formed with one another. In a world where one-night stands and brief liaisons were commonplace, women in committed relationships often sought out other stable couples. It cut down on the drama, the flirting, the illicit passes at someone else's date.

These friendships allowed the couples to relax and get to know one another inside out. They socialized together, vacationed together, and tended to freak out if one of the pairs broke up. The intact couple usually embraced the injured party—the woman who got dumped—and found it hard to maintain contact with the one who strayed.

At least that had been Amanda's experience when she got dumped by Rachel Lessing, the only long-term partner in her life, and although she had not stuck around in Sarasota long enough to find out if her old friends would embrace her, she knew one thing with absolute certainty: when the dumpee brought a new girlfriend into the old mix, there could be all hell to pay. The new woman would be measured by the old standard, constantly compared to the one who had strayed, and she loathed being that odd woman out.

"This break will do you good," Mom insisted as she helped Amanda pack. "And don't worry, Matthew and I will be fine with Lissa until Ginny gets home."

Mom knew she and Ginny had become best friends, and now that Ginny was married, she feared Amanda would get lonesome. "You need to expand your social circle, Mandy, and women friends are essential, a support system for life."

*Right, Mom. If you only knew!*

Mom was so excited she even took Amanda shopping for a new, one-piece swimsuit. "This will work until that ugly scar from the bullet heals. Don't worry, honey, you'll be back in your bikini before you know it."

Her mother was not a confidence builder. Sara had seen Amanda naked only once, pre-scar. Amanda knew the imperfection would not dampen Sara's ardor one little bit, but she hated for the other women to see her winter-white legs. On its best day, her fair skin was not beach-friendly. If she didn't slather up with stinky sunscreen, cover her exposed limbs, or shelter under an umbrella, she would be a lobster-red blister by day two.

"Look, your friends are here, honey!" Mom was thrilled when a new burgundy Subaru Outback pulled into their driveway.

Amanda was petrified. So she put a brave smile frozen on her lips as the trio emerged from the car. Sara climbed out from the backseat. She looked relaxed and amazing in raggedy cutoff jeans and a faded green Outer Banks T-shirt. When she took Amanda into her open arms and kissed her cheek, Amanda wondered if Mom was watching. Had she seen the shiny rainbow flag decal on the bumper? Did she even know what it meant?

"Don't be shy, you two," Sara urged her friends. "Step up and meet Mandy."

The Cat Couple had been hanging back, with sunglasses hiding their expressions. They did not look like cats—or maybe one of them did. The first to come forward was an erect, tall, elegant African American woman, with a liquid stride that was indeed cat-like. Her limbs were as long and smooth as the caramel Sugar Daddy candies-on-a-stick Amanda used to buy at the Jersey Shore.

"Amanda Rittenhouse, meet Maya Hunter."

Maya's fingers were cool as she shook Amanda's hand. Her close-cropped Afro glistened, while her full lips and ultra-white teeth opened in a warm smile. At the same time, she seemed surprised as she continued to gape at her.

"And this is Sharon Williams. We all call her Shar." Sara pronounced the nickname like the word *"are"* with a *"sh"* in front.

Shar was white, medium height, with very curly, jaw-length brown hair, big chocolate eyes, and a bosom to rival Dolly Parton's. She, too, seemed to be staring.

"Pleased to meet you, Mandy." Her southern accent was warm honey.

The two were an unlikely pair, but what did Amanda know? She had wanted to have an open mind when she met them, so she had deliberately asked no questions. She gave them clumsy little hugs, and then Sara helped her load her gear in through the hatchback.

For the first fifty miles, Sara was unusually chatty. Maybe she, too, was nervous about adding Amanda to the inner circle. She seemed determined to recite Amanda's résumé from how they had met at Metrolina, to how she had lived in Philadelphia, then Sarasota, and now Mooresville. She gave an exaggeratedly glowing testimony to Amanda's skills as a metal sculptor. The litany made Amanda blush. Luckily Sara didn't mention the murder mystery that had featured in their first weeks together.

Maya and Shar paid attention, made all the right noises, and commented on the high points. But all the while, Amanda wondered how her biography compared to that of Sara's ex, the mysterious Judith Dillinger.

Finally, she interrupted. "Hey, enough about me. Tell me about you guys."

Maya objected. "Sara will be bored to death."

"So will you, Mandy." Shar offered a playful wink.

Nonetheless, people can't resist talking about themselves, so over the next hundred miles, she learned she and Maya Hunter had something in common. "Wow, I can't believe you grew up in Philly too! Did your mom really teach at Girls' High? That's the best public school in the city!" And Maya's father was a city councilman, a highly respected elected official whom Amanda's parents had voted for.

"Maya is an assistant district attorney in Charlotte," Sara added. "I met her at the ADA's office. She jails many of the juvies who eventually end up as my clients."

"Right. I put those punks in prison, and then Sara makes sure they don't go back."

"I try," Sara commented ruefully.

Amanda wondered how much the Cat Couple knew about their current mission to Hatteras. Had Maya ever prosecuted Tammy Tillman?

"Well, *I* met Sara at a little boutique I own called Goddess Gifts." Shar giggled. "Sara came in to buy some lesbian romance literature and I gave her a really hard time. See, Maya had told me who she was, but Sara had no idea I was Maya's significant other. The rest is history."

As the three began describing the delights sold in Shar's store—everything from candles to healing crystals—Amanda's mind wandered. The only person's résumé conspicuously missing was Judith's. This was to be expected since Sara's lover was the one who'd defected, but Amanda was dying to know everything about her.

She knew from Sara's twin brother, Marc, that the breakup between Sara and Jude had been dramatic and devastating. She knew from Sara herself that she had been terribly hurt. In fact, after their one passionate night together, Sara had said, "I don't do relationships," and Amanda suspected Sara had been badly burned. Still, going forward she had to find out if Sara's shredded trust could be mended. If so, she wanted to be the one to do it.

Part of the answer came when the quartet stopped for lunch at a hole-in the-wall local restaurant called "EATS". Maya and Sara strolled ahead laughing, while Shar lagged behind to help Amanda dig her sunglasses out of her pull-along.

She took advantage of the opportunity. "Listen, Shar," she whispered. "Can you tell me a little something about Sara's ex, Judith?"

Shar stared at her and seemed to consider her options. Finally, she smiled and crossed her arms over her astonishing bosom. "Well, doll, I'll tell you one thing, and it shocked the hell out of me. You and Jude? You look exactly alike."

# CHAPTER TEN

*Windswept silk...*

The insight that Amanda closely resembled Sara's ex was troubling. All through lunch and the next leg of the journey, even when Sara quietly took her hand and they touched knees in the backseat, Amanda questioned Sara's motives. Had Sara been attracted to her for her unique qualities, or was she looking for a Jude substitute? She tried to remain upbeat and engaged in the lively conversation, but the blue funk continued until they reached the Alligator River National Wildlife Refuge on the mainland, then crossed the first big bridge to Roanoke Island. At that point she forgot to be upset and allowed the amazing landscape to seduce her.

"This is where it all began," Maya thrilled. "We are in Dare County, named for Virginia Dare, the first child born in the Americas to English parents. This is the home of the Lost Colony, the ghost deer, and the bloody pirate, Blackbeard."

Shar sighed and rolled her eyes. "Watch out, Mandy. My mate here is an expert on the local legends, and what's worse, she believes them. Get ready for spooky stories every night. Maya loves to scare us to death before we go to bed."

"Well, the Outer Banks *is* the Graveyard of the Atlantic," Sara added. "Thousands have perished at sea after their ships wrecked on the treacherous shoals, or the pirates lured them aground and slaughtered them. Really, Mandy, it's safer not to sleep with all those ghosts about." Sara's naughty look implied they'd not be doing much sleeping, ghosts or not.

By then, traffic had slowed to almost a standstill as summer travelers lined up at the bridge to cross Roanoke Sound to Bodic Island. After crossing, Amanda noticed that most cars turned south on NC Highway 12, the narrowly paved road with the Atlantic to the east and Pamlico Sound to the west. The women explained that the thin broken strand connected the islands of Bodie, Hatteras, and Ocracoke, each with its own lighthouse. It passed through eight villages that reflected the island's history and remained independent of Cape Hatteras National Seashore, which the federal government maintained.

Maya frowned at the traffic. "Whose bright idea was it to change our lovely, quiet fall vacation to a summer event?"

Shar rubbed the short burr of Maya's hair. "C'mon, it'll be an adventure. Maybe Sara and Mandy will let us help solve the Tammy mystery. Besides, you're a people-watcher. Just think about all those half-naked girls on the beach."

Maya grumbled. "I'd rather share the sand with the shells and the shipwrecks."

The sheer majesty of endless waves pounding the beach beyond the towering dunes mesmerized Amanda. She rolled down her window, heard the surf and smelled the salt. She was no stranger to the ocean. As a child, her family took vacations to the Jersey Shore, and as an adult, she and Rachel had lived only blocks from the aqua-green Gulf of Mexico.

Magical as those were, the primal, unspoiled essence of the Banks was entirely different. Even with cars clogging the beach-access lots and humanity swarming the shore, it was clear who was boss here. The mighty ocean reigned supreme. People were the vulnerable interlopers on this precarious, seventy-mile-long string that bellowed out from the mainland. It was connected north and south, but completely at the mercy of the sea, the winds, the tides, and the storms. The farther south they drove, the more Amanda sensed the elemental isolation that humbled mere humans in the face of God Nautilus.

"It must get lonely here in the winter," she mused aloud.

"Jude and I came here once in winter," Sara responded, a faraway look in her eyes. "We rented a little trailer and stayed 'til the money ran out. Most of the restaurants and shops were closed, but we still had a grocery store, and the Bankers were kind to us. They are a hardy lot."

"The year Mom bought the condo where we'll be staying, we came down for Christmas," Shar added. "It was strange to see colored lights strung up in the little towns. And what was really weird—they celebrated what they call 'Old Christmas' on January sixth."

"Why?" Sara wondered.

"They believe in Old Buck, a beast that brings the villager's dead ancestors back for that day," Maya explained. "Old Buck lives in Trent Woods near Rodanthe and shows himself only on Old Christmas. He looks like a medieval hobbyhorse. In present-day celebrations a man carries a piece of wood shaped like a horse's head and neck, and he makes its mouth snap open and shut."

"See, I told you Maya knows it all," Shar said.

"Well, I saw a movie called *Nights in Rodanthe*. It was really romantic, with Richard Gere," Amanda said.

"It was a stupid movie, and Diane Lane was the romantic one," Sara corrected her. "But I did enjoy that amazing house being torn apart by the storm."

"That house from the movie is right down that road." Maya pointed.

As they passed through Waves, Salvo, Avon, and stopped at a grocery in Buxton, Amanda realized the place was seducing her. After the long day of travel, the frisson of sexual tension between herself and Sara, combined with the heady sea air in her lungs, soothed and excited her as they neared their destination.

She had offered to pay her share of the condo rent until Shar explained that her mom had given them the place free of charge. Apparently Shar came from a wealthy family, because

Amanda had also learned that Shar's father had given her the seed money for her shop, Goddess Gifts.

"You can chip in on the food, though," Maya suggested. "Or you and Sara can buy what you like, and Shar and I can choose our stuff."

"Just so we buy plenty of fresh seafood," Amanda said as they entered the store.

But her suggestion was met with cold stares of incredulity by the other couple. "Don't you remember? Shar and I are deathly allergic to shellfish," Maya said.

"Sorry. Maybe *Sara's Jude* remembered your allergy, but *I* do not," Amanda grumbled, but then quickly modified her tone. "But we'll all enjoy plenty of wine, right?"

"Maya and Shar don't drink," Sara whispered as she took her aside. "But hey, that won't stop us. We'll get our own seafood and wine and enjoy whatever we want on this vacation."

It was not an auspicious beginning, Amanda decided as they divided into couples and pushed two separate carts up and down the aisles. Again she felt like the outsider. She was completely unschooled in the habits of this foursome, the new cog in an old wheel.

Once they were back on the road, they entered a little town called Frisco and turned off the highway toward the ocean. "Aren't we going to Hatteras? That's where Tammy's mother lives."

"Hatteras is just down the road, but Shar's place is here. You'll really love it, babe," Sara said as they pulled into a carport under a two-storied structure constructed of weathered gray clapboard.

Much to her delight, the tall modern building was right on the ocean with only a pair of low dune foothills between them and the crashing surf. "This is awesome!" she cried.

"Roll up your windows quick before the mosquitos fly into the car," Maya warned. "And don't worry, the wind will blow the little buggers away as we climb upward."

Huffing like packhorses under the weight of suitcases and groceries, they had to make several trips up and down the steep flights of stairs, which actually swayed slightly in the wind as they ascended. Amanda knew these buildings were built on stilts so floods and hurricanes would not destroy them, but the moving timbers were unsettling.

"You'll get used to it," Sara promised. "We'll be like little squirrels in a nest, rocked to sleep each night in our treetop."

Luckily the three bedrooms and two full baths were on the first floor, so each couple chose a bedroom with a queen bed, then deposited their luggage in the third room, which had bunkbeds.

The upper floor was the living area. It was so spectacular that Amanda gasped in appreciation. The entire glass front wall opened onto a full deck with a panoramic view of the Atlantic. As far as the eye could see, ocean, dunes, and dramatic sunset clouds made up the horizon. The floorplan was completely open with pale natural tones on the few walls, sand-colored Berber carpet, a modern kitchen with a picnic table in the rear, and comfortable sofas and chairs grouped around a driftwood coffee table.

Sara came up behind her and pulled her close. "Will it do?"

"It will do very nicely." She melted backward into her arms.

Everyone agreed the search for Tammy Tillman could wait until tomorrow, and after that, the evening unfolded like windswept silk. She and Sara had drinks on the deck, while Maya and Shar cooked a feast of native croaker fish, baked potatoes, and roasted Brussel sprouts, with key lime pie for dessert. Afterward, they were too tired to start a jigsaw puzzle. Maya even lacked the strength to tell a ghost story, so they turned in early.

After showering, and still very shy with one another, they slipped into their nest. While the wind rocked their cradle, but before they kissed, Amanda asked, "Shar told me I look exactly like Jude. Is that true?"

Sara reared up on one elbow, her green eyes shifting with a combination of surprise and desire. "No, babe. You may look like her, but you are nothing like her. She was the dark of night, you are the light of day."

# CHAPTER ELEVEN

*I am the booty...*

Amanda awoke feeling languorous, luxuriant, and sore in all the right places. Their lovemaking had been slower, sweeter, but even more satisfying than the first time around. Three months ago life had intervened, causing them to wait. The delay had somehow intensified the climax, leaving her stunned and surprised by her body's hungry reaction. With her ex, sex had been serious and intense, but with Sara it was playful and fun. Her orgasm was beyond anything she had ever experienced.

As promised, their nest had swayed ever so slightly and the sound of the surf was their lullaby as the breeze from the open window caressed, chilled, and dried the taste of salt on their skin. She didn't want to get up, but Sara had already left their bed with a parting kiss. She had showered, dressed, and ascended to the main floor.

She did want to open her eyes to discover how the haunting seascape she'd witnessed at dawn, when she'd snuck out of bed for a bathroom break, had changed with the light of day. Just before sunrise, the old Frisco Fishing Pier, a local landmark, had shimmered in brilliant contrast with the shifting dark blues and grays. The women had told her that in 2010, Hurricane Earl trashed the wooden dock leading out to the pier, but the huge, long, low building remained intact. Its bright yellow walls seemed to glow from within, dramatic in predawn. The only odd thing she'd seen as night turned to day were lights bobbing on the beach.

Now, after pulling on a T-shirt and crossing stiffly to the window, she was surprised to see the parking lot behind the fishing pier already filled with cars and the beach dotted with people. *At eight in the morning?* She had better get with the program. Indeed, by the time she went upstairs, Shar was already clearing breakfast dishes.

"Sorry I'm late. Where is everyone?"

Shar smiled and nodded out at the deck. "Sara's trying to talk one of her patients down off a ledge, and Maya's already out shelling."

Sara was pacing, her cell phone to her ear, a cup of coffee in the other hand. When she turned and caught sight of Amanda, her smile eclipsed the sun.

"Has Sara eaten breakfast yet?"

"She's waiting for you."

Amanda commandeered the frying pan Shar was rinsing. She dried it and began heating it for scrambled eggs. She sliced some French bread, slathered it with butter, and placed it in the toaster oven. Whether Sara was hungry or not, she needed food, and Amanda intended to cook for them both. After their performances during the night, they were running on empty.

She turned to Shar. "I saw lights out on the beach last night. Doesn't anyone sleep around here?"

Shar blinked. "That's funny. It's illegal to visit the beach at night. I'm surprised someone didn't call the cops."

All this was news to her. "You say Maya's out shelling?"

"Yep, she's a fanatic. She claims the best specimens wash up with the tide, so she always wants first shot at the pickings." Shar lifted a mug from the cupboard. "Want some tea?"

"No thanks, I'm a coffee gal." Without her caffeine fix, she'd not only wilt by noon, she'd also suffer a major headache.

"Really? Jude used to drink tea," Shar said.

"Well, lucky for me, Sara's a coffee gal too." There it was again, another comparison to the ex-girlfriend. "You said I look like Jude, but what was she like? What made her tick?"

Shar ran fingers through her curly brown hair and smiled at Amanda. "Look, I didn't mean to imply you had a personality like Jude. Hell, she was a jock. You're an artist. She taught political science and coached the women's tennis team at Queen's University in Charlotte. Maybe Sara didn't tell you, but Jude left her for a biology teacher who also worked there."

"Sara hasn't told me anything," she admitted as she broke four eggs into a bowl and added a dollop of Worcestershire sauce and milk.

"Don't worry about it, doll. I'm sure she doesn't want to talk about it, but I'll tell you one thing…" She laid a warm hand on her arm. "Jude had a dark nature. She brought Sara down. You're so much better for her, trust me."

The unexpected vote of confidence almost brought tears to her eyes. "Thanks," she gulped.

"Are you guys talking about me?" Suddenly Sara was in the room.

"Weren't your ears burning?" Shar winked at Amanda.

"Yes, they were, but the one responsible was the ex-felon I was talking to on the phone. Now, I promise to leave the clinic behind."

"Good idea." Amanda gave her a shy little kiss on the cheek. "The only one of your patients I want to know about on this vacation is Tammy, and maybe we can find her quickly."

"You bet, right after breakfast."

Shar left to join Maya before Sara and Amanda finished their eggs. She wore a swimsuit, shorts, flip-flops, and carried a tote bag big enough for several pounds of seashells.

"Is that bag for the booty?" Amanda asked.

Shar turned on the way out the door, cupped her bodacious breasts in both hands and gave them a playful jiggle. "I am the booty, doll, and don't you forget it."

# CHAPTER TWELVE

*Queen of the Mer-Maids...*

Lynette Tillman's house in Hatteras proved to be nothing like they expected. Having experienced her daughter Tammy's place in mill town, they assumed the mother would live in one of the unpretentious cottages or trailers inhabited by many of the locals. Not so.

As they neared the address listed in Tammy's file, they entered a tony neighborhood just off Pamlico Sound where rich summer folks had built expensive mansions in the distinctive Outer Banks style—charming, multistoried wooden structures sporting multiple decks, covered porches, decorative porthole windows—all painted in bright, joyful colors.

"Are you sure we're in the right place?" Amanda wondered.

Sara steered Maya's new Outback onto a waterfront street and parked in front of a jaunty shingle-shake home painted tan with blue trim. "Yes, this is it. I wonder how Mrs. Tillman made the money to afford this?" She turned to her. "By the way, did you ever get anything from Tammy's cell phone?"

"Afraid not. I got the damned thing charged, but it's still dead. I think it needs a new battery. Any chance of getting one out here on the island?"

"Good luck with that."

Feeling suddenly nervous because of their unannounced intrusion, she followed a few paces behind Sara, up a walkway through a neat rock garden planted with colorful perennials. When Sara lifted the brass doorbell shaped like an anchor, they heard a nautical hornpipe play inside.

"Maybe she's not home?" Amanda said hopefully.

"Nope, she's coming."

The door swung inward, opened by a little towheaded boy about six years old. "Who are you?" he demanded.

Both were taken aback, especially when a scowling teenage girl, also blond, inched up behind him.

"Is your mother home?" Sara asked tentatively.

"Who wants to know?" the girl said.

"Please tell your mother that Dr. Sara Orlando is here. I spoke to her last week about Tammy."

Both children's eyes grew enormous. The girl guarded the door while the boy ran to deliver the news.

"Is Tammy your sister?" Sara continued.

"Tammy's a whore. We don't talk about her."

Sara looked as shocked as she was. Amanda knew Tammy had a history of drug abuse and theft—but prostitution? Also, Sara had never mentioned Tammy had younger siblings. Maybe she'd never told her?

The boy returned dragging a middle-aged woman by the hand. She was a short, wiry, dishwater blonde—the spitting image of her daughter, except for the deep worry lines etched on her face and the liver spots on her hands. Amanda glanced at her inner arms—no signs of needle marks. Either she was injecting elsewhere or she had given up heroin.

"I told you on the phone. My good-for-nothing daughter's not here," Lynette Tillman said without preamble.

"Yes, but may we come in? I'd like to ask you a few questions."

"I haven't seen her in two years."

Somehow Sara got her foot in the door. "This is my friend, Mandy. Mind if she listens in?"

If Lynette had minded, it was irrelevant, because Sara was already marching down the hall toward the kitchen, everyone else in tow. Amanda admired her courage, or was it chutzpah?

"What do you want?" Lynette snapped. She turned to the children raiding the fridge, helping themselves to sodas. "You two get lost! Go to your room until these ladies leave."

Surprisingly they obeyed immediately. Sara had mentioned Tammy's mother was physically abusive, so likely the kids expected a smack upside the head if they didn't hop to.

"I hate Sundays, with the damned kids underfoot all day," Lynette grumbled. "Tomorrow they'll be back at summer day school, thank God."

Once they were alone, Lynette flopped into a chair at the oval table but did not invite them to join her. Sara sat anyway, so Amanda followed suit. She saw a pot of fresh coffee, but Lynette did not offer them a cup.

"Well?"

Sara laid it all out. She told the woman about Tammy's disappearance.

Amanda jumped right in and described Sonny Roach's likely role in causing her to run. "He thinks she hid some money."

Lynette barked out a derisive laugh. "Sonny told me the bitch stole over five thousand dollars from him. I know he went to Mooresville to get it back. Who can blame him?"

Lynette's use of the English language disintegrated as the interview progressed, and her diction became more slurred as she sipped the coffee. Amanda saw a bottle of vodka near the sink and suspected the coffee was spiked.

"So how would Tammy steal money from Sonny if she hasn't been home in years?" Amanda pressed.

"Sonny Roach is a rich man. He owns a towing company here on the island. He has more than ten trucks in his fleet and serves the whole Outer Banks," Lynette bragged, not answering the question.

"I understand, but when did your daughter steal the money?"

Amanda's relentless technique finally rattled the woman.

"I never said she ain't been in town. I said she ain't been *here*, in this house. She ain't welcome here."

"That's a surprise," Sara said. "Tammy has never missed a counseling session. She must have been sneaking down here between sessions, and that's a parole violation."

"She comes to see her asshole boyfriend. She stays with him, not me."

Sara and Amanda gaped at one another. *Boyfriend?*

"What's the boyfriend's name?" Sara asked.

"She calls him Rusty. He's the same stupid redhead she dated in high school."

Lynette didn't know Rusty's last name, where he worked, or where he lived. She did know he was "not worth spit on the sidewalk." Before the interview slid completely downhill, Amanda changed the subject.

"This is a lovely home, Mrs. Tillman. What do you do for a living?"

Lynette's scrawny chest puffed with pride. "I own my own business, a cleaning service. It's called Island Mer-Maids. Ain't that cute? I bet you seen my cars around town—yellow Kia Souls with a mermaid on the side. The mermaid's using her tail like a broom."

Amanda couldn't even think of a response as she stared at the queen of the Mer-Maids.

"Like Sonny, I have maids working the whole island. We clean most of the vacation rentals between customers."

Sara said, "You two sound really successful. Do you know where I can find Sonny? I'd like to speak to him."

Lynette changed from a moderately drunk hostess to an extremely angry hellion. She got alarmingly red in the face, her blue eyes focused and sparked, and her small hands clenched.

"Sonny ain't here. I ain't seen him, neither."

Amanda thought the lady doth protest too much, and as Lynette marched them to the front door, all pretense of civility ended, and her suspicions were confirmed. Sonny's distinctive alligator boots were sitting side by side on the floor, outside the bedroom door.

# CHAPTER THIRTEEN

*I left him on his own...*

Maya and Shar chose a restaurant on the waterfront. After their long day at the beach, Shar was pink with sunburn, Maya's brown skin was mahogany-red, and everyone was too tired to cook.

"Hey, you guys worked today while we played," Maya said. "So tonight we're treating—anything you want."

"Good deal." Sara grinned and ordered a margarita.

Amanda asked for a rum and tonic. "Did you find some nice shells?"

"Oh yeah, I got some great ones for the store. I made Maya search for small ones with a hole for a chain so I can make them into jewelry. My customers love earrings and necklaces."

"I hope we can help with the shelling tomorrow," Sara said wistfully. "Today was a wild-goose chase."

"Right," Amanda added. "After Lynette Tillman tossed us out of her house, we drove aimlessly around looking for Tammy and a redheaded guy who might be her boyfriend. Then we stopped at a local branch of the Dare County Sheriff's Office in Buxton and found a redhead there."

Sara laughed. "Yeah, Deputy Mike Doyle. We told him Tammy's story and asked if the local authorities could keep an eye out for her, but he thought we were crazy. He didn't even take one note."

"Well, what did you expect?" Maya said. "Tammy's an adult, and you have no proof she's in trouble. Why don't you two forget about it and enjoy your vacation?"

Amanda knew this was good advice, so for the moment, she shook off her worries and let the soothing ambiance of the restaurant—white walls, dark wood tables, gently spinning ceiling fans—seduce her. It was impossible to stay uptight while looking out the big picture window at the narrow harbor, with sand and sea filling the horizon. So she relaxed and enjoyed the gentle pressure of Sara's bare arm against hers, the subtle spice of her perfume, and the girls' chatter as they explained why they were the Cat Couple.

"We have four permanent feline family members," Maya said, "and an ongoing procession of fosters. Right now we're hosting a young mother and her four kittens. At the time we left, the kittens had diarrhea and Mama was in heat. Needless to say, it wasn't a great time to go on vacation."

Amanda's mind wandered while Shar described the various catsitters they'd used over the years, but when they discussed different brands of kitty litter, she completely tuned out in favor of savoring her seafood marinara. The couple finished talking about their animal kingdom, the conversation drifted back to Lynette Tillman.

Shar said, "I've seen those Island Mer-Maids cars. This afternoon I left Maya on the beach and came back to get another shell bag. While I was there, some guy drove up in one."

Maya lifted her dark eyebrows. "Some *guy*? You'd think all the maids would be women."

"No, it was a man, but he wasn't there to clean our house. He was servicing the hot tub out on the deck. He told me they check the chlorine levels and switches between rental guests just to be sure it's working properly."

"Hear that, girls?" Shar shook her booty and grinned. "Now we can all get naked and party in the hot tub."

Amanda groaned. So far she'd avoided showing off her winter-white legs, not to mention her scar, but it seemed the inevitable was looming.

"So did he fix it?" Sara glanced suggestively in her direction.

"I guess so," Shar said. "I didn't stick around to find out. You guys had gone on your sleuthing mission, and Maya was still down on the beach, so I left him on his own."

"How did he get in?" Amanda asked.

"He didn't need to get inside, silly. The outside stairs tie into the deck, remember? He just hauled his tools up that way and I left him to it."

Amanda and Sara ordered coffee, Shar and Maya asked for tea, and soon the waiter brought their bill. They all waited, pretending not to notice as Maya dug through her purse, becoming progressively more agitated with each pass.

"I must have left my wallet back at the condo," she said at last.

"Don't worry, doll, I'll get it." Shar dragged her bag from under her chair and rooted inside. The seconds ticked slowly as Shar went through the same process, turning alarmingly red as she searched. "I can't believe it, but my wallet is missing too, and I know damn well it was in my bag when I left for the beach this morning."

"You both left your purses at the house? Are you sure you locked the door?" Sara asked.

"Absolutely!" Shar snapped. "Shit, my credit cards, driver's license, social security card—everything was in my wallet!"

"Fuck! Everything was in mine too! Including my ADA pocket card. It costs a small fortune to replace that license, so I'm screwed." Maya was embarrassed. If a blush could be detected under her dark skin, it would have burned through her flesh.

"No problem, I'll pay and we'll settle up later." Amanda quickly slid her Visa into the little black folder.

But Maya couldn't contain her distress. "Thanks, Mandy. I know it's Sunday night, but can you take us back to the sheriff's office you visited this afternoon?"

# CHAPTER FOURTEEN

*Tulip…*

"So why do you blame the hot-tub guy? You said he never went inside, and you locked the door when you left, right?"

Deputy Mike Doyle was still on duty when the four of them trooped into the office. He was tired, near the end of his shift, and running on strong coffee, but he still seemed as young and clueless as he had that afternoon when Amanda and Sara gave him the lowdown on their search for Tammy. Sara, who routinely dealt with rookie cops, even counseled them as patients, had called Deputy Doyle "Baby Face," and not just because of his smooth pink cheeks, blue eyes, and perfectly combed red hair. It was because he lacked the imagination to visualize the serious trouble a girl like Tammy could be in with a man like Sonny Roach.

Doyle had admitted to knowing Sonny and labeled him a "harmless badass." It seemed Sonny had a reputation on the island as a womanizer and an occasionally nasty drunk, but the success he'd made of his towing business was universally respected. He even had a contract with the Dare County Sheriff's Department to rescue their squad cars in distress.

Tonight the deputy had actually sighed when Amanda and Sara reappeared, this time with Shar and Maya. He had initially eyed them all with mild irritation. Amanda couldn't decide if Doyle thought they were a nuisance or if he was homophobic. Either way, his attitude improved when he understood the women had been robbed.

"Of course I locked the damn door," Shar repeated. "Also, we had both hidden our purses in a dresser drawer before we left. We never leave our valuables in plain sight when we travel."

"You two always travel together?"

This time Amanda was certain the deputy was less homophobic, more like he had a prurient interest in what women did in bed together. Possibly the fact Shar and Maya were a mixed-race couple made the speculation even more titillating.

"Please listen carefully, Deputy. The door was locked. I noticed no sign of forced entry when we returned from the beach, so I'm guessing the thief had a key," Maya said, every inch the prosecutor.

Her tone woke the kid up. He sat up straight and took a nervous sip of coffee. "Well, you're right, ma'am. We've had a rash of these identity thefts lately. Mostly seems to happen to tourists because Bankers know to keep their money close."

"While we *tourists*, on the other hand, flaunt our cash and beg to get robbed?" Maya was steamed. "Shar told you the hot-tub guy arrived in an Island Mer-Maids car. What about that?"

Mike Doyle blushed. "Sure, I know the company. It's owned by Lynette Tillman, the woman you met this morning." He nodded at Amanda and Sara. "Like I told you before, Lynette's good people. The Mer-Maids clean for folks all up and down the Outer Banks."

So naturally, Amanda thought, these good people were beyond reproach. She turned to Shar. "Your mom owns the building where we're staying. Does she employ the Mer-Maids to clean up for her?"

Shar shrugged. "I doubt if Mom knows anything about it. A property management company handles all that."

Doyle asked the name of the management company and wrote it down. It was the first note Amanda had seen him take all day.

"So that will be easy to check, right?" she asked him.

He nodded vigorously. "I'm sure we'll get to the bottom of this."

Amanda and Sara glanced at one another, both completely lacking confidence in the kid's ability to get to the bottom of his own pocket as he fumbled through a desk drawer. Eventually he came up with two identical forms, which he flattened on the counter in front of Shar and Maya. "Please list everything that was inside your wallets, including a description of the wallets themselves."

The girls rolled their eyes. "This could take time," Shar said.

"Okay, we'll wait outside." Sara nodded at the door.

Amanda and Sara exited the building and stood in the parking lot, gulping the fresh night air, which had a salty tang like the rim of a margarita glass.

"What do you think? Will Baby Face catch the bad guys?" Sara asked.

"Sure he will—when pigs fly and the oceans run dry."

They settled on a concrete bench and secretly held hands, grateful that the mosquitos had not yet found them. Sara said, "Too bad. So far our vacation's been a disaster. Plus, not having credit cards will really cramp the girls' style. It'll be hell notifying all the banks to close their accounts."

"Not necessarily. I lost a card once, and Wells Fargo sent me a new one the very next day. By Wednesday they should be able to shop 'til they drop."

"I hope it works out that way, but I wish Shar could remember the hot-tub guy's name. Maybe he has a criminal record?"

Amanda realized Sara felt responsible, since the unscheduled vacation had been her idea. "Cheer up. I don't know about you, but I'm having a great time. Soon we'll be back in our treetop nest." She leaned into Sara but then reflexively moved away when a black-and-white patrol car marked *K9 Unit* pulled into the lot and parked right beside them.

As they watched, a beautiful woman in a tan uniform climbed out, smiled, and then opened the rear hatch of her unit. The officer reminded Amanda of Sara—same compact stature, generous curves, perfect skin—but her shorter black hair was pulled back in a tight ponytail and her eyes were not amazingly green like Sara's. Her nametag said *P. Aqua*.

"Are you guys afraid of dogs?" She gave them a probing once-over.

"We love dogs!" Amanda replied.

"Okay, then. Come Tulip!" She gave a short, sharp whistle and a sleek, powerful German shepherd leaped gracefully to the concrete wearing a substantial harness with an actual gold sheriff's star pinned to the chest strap.

"You call him *Tulip*?" Sara was incredulous.

Officer Aqua laughed. "I call *her* Tulip, because she comes from Holland and she's sooo pretty." She scratched Tulip between her two pointy ears. In turn Tulip smiled and her tongue hung out.

"You get your service dogs from Holland?" Sara asked.

"Yes, we do. Only the best for Dare County. Our dogs get their basic training there, and then we handlers fly over and pick our partners. We finish the training at home."

"Where does Tulip live?" Amanda asked.

"She lives with me. She's part of the family."

"May I pet her?"

The officer touched the dog's shoulder and Tulip sat, staring eagerly at them. "Sure, go ahead."

Not needing a second invitation, Sara and Amanda stroked Tulip's fur, while Officer Aqua explained that her partner was not always so docile. She was a drug-sniffer, tracker, and cadaver dog, and capable of an on-command attack that could bring down the toughest thug.

"By the way, I'm Sergeant Paula Aqua." She held out a strong tanned hand. "I know, people always do a double-take when they hear the name Aqua, which means 'dweller by the water' in Spanish. It's just a coincidence, believe me, because all my ancestors were land-locked farmers."

"I guess folks don't forget your name, Sergeant Aqua," Sara said.

Amanda guessed folks didn't forget much about her, and suddenly Amanda was speculating about whether or not Paula Aqua might be gay. From Sara's piqued interest, she realized with a tiny twitch of jealousy that Sara was wondering the same thing. In her experience, Paula would give them some sort of a signal if this was true.

"So what brings you to the sheriff's office? Anything I can help you with?"

Somehow as they continued to maul Tulip, the whole story came out—from Tammy's disappearance to the identity theft. Sergeant Aqua pulled out a pad and took a few notes.

"Sorry to hear about all this, but Deputy Doyle will do a good job for your friends. He's young, but he's ambitious. He won't let it slide."

Before they could argue, Shar and Maya appeared. For a Cat Couple, they, too, went gaga for Tulip.

"Are you relieving Deputy Doyle now?" Shar eyed Aqua with interest.

"Nope. We close the office up for the night now. Mike gets to go home, but Tulip and I get to patrol the beach. Early this morning some folks in Frisco saw lights down on the dunes, so we'll check it out."

"I saw those lights too. What's going on?" Amanda asked.

"Drugs, maybe." Aqua was guarded. "This summer the Outer Banks has been under siege from a pretty sophisticated distribution network. One theory is that the product comes ashore in small boats, but I think that's nuts. My lieutenant's been reading too many pirate stories."

"Kids maybe?" Sara offered.

"Most likely teenagers smoking pot and playing house. Don't worry about it."

Amanda was more worried about the admiring look Sara was bestowing upon the lovely Sergeant Aqua. "I bet you hate working the night shift," she said.

"Yes, I do." Aqua smiled knowingly. "But my partner, Jo, hates it even more. She'll throw me out of the house if it goes on much longer."

Ah-ha. The clue! And not so subtle, at that.

They all gaped as the sergeant and Tulip went into the office. She waved at them. "Bye, guys. Maybe I'll see you around."

# CHAPTER FIFTEEN

*Cold drinks and sandwiches...*

Monday morning was sunny and clear, exactly like the day before except everyone switched roles. Amanda was up first while Sara slept in. They'd all turned in early, too tired for ghost stories or hot tubs, and again she and Sara made sweet love. Again she was sore and satisfied in all the right places, but she was sleepy as well. Once Sara had fallen asleep, Amanda had crept to the window and watched for lights on the beach. And she'd seen them—not several bobbing beams like the night before, but only one. She figured it was Sergeant Aqua.

The officer's nocturnal tactics had been fascinating to watch. She would shelter for fifteen minutes behind one hummock of sand, then switch on her flashlight and scamper to a different vantage point farther down the beach. Once Amanda thought she heard a dog whine, but it could have been the wind, and she never caught sight of the patrol car. Paula Aqua seemed to be having a slow, unproductive night, so Amanda had soon gone back to bed.

"You're up early, Mandy," Maya commented as she and Shar joined her on the top level. Both were casually dressed for a day on the town.

"Already on my second cup of coffee," Amanda bragged.

Shar grinned. "Did you wear Sara out last night? She's usually the early bird."

"No comment." She blushed. "So where are you two girls off to?"

Shar put on the teakettle and poured some healthful-looking granola into bowls for herself and Maya. "Believe it or not, I've already had a call from my bank. They wanted to know why I had purchased a thousand dollars' worth of golf clubs online and then shipped them to Boise, Idaho."

"No shit, what did you do?"

"Well, I agreed with them that the activity did not fit my shopping pattern, told them what happened, and asked them to cancel the damn card."

"Luckily Shar has fraud insurance," Maya explained. "Bank of America will forgive the debt and try to run down the perpetrators. They'll even put out an all-points bulletin on all her cards from other banks and give them a head's-up to stop honoring purchases."

"Good deal. I hope you have insurance, too, Maya," Amanda said.

"No, I was too stupid to bother. I prosecute identity thieves all the time, so you'd think I'd take precautions, but unfortunately when someone buys a state-of-the-art entertainment center on one of my cards, I may have to eat the loss."

"Maybe not," Shar said. "We're going over to the hotel, where they have public Internet and a printing facility. Maya can DocuSign all the paperwork, fax stuff, whatever needs to be done. With any luck, we'll head off a disaster."

"I'll be rooting for you." Amanda watched them gulp tea. "Sara and I are spending the day on the beach. Maybe we'll find some good shells for you, Shar."

"Thanks. And you can wish us luck at the sheriff's, too, because in the middle of the night I remembered the hot-tub guy's first name. It was Eddie."

"Did his name just come to you?"

"Power of association. At the time, the man reminded me of this old heartthrob singer my grandma used to love. He had the same dimples, same curly dark hair—like Eddie Fisher."

Amanda loved Shar's goofy reasoning. It occurred to her as the women waved their goodbyes, that in a few short days she felt close to this couple. Somehow she was no longer the outsider, and she hoped with all her heart that their friendship would deepen and endure.

"Maybe trauma makes the heart grow fonder?" Sara suggested as they strolled at water's edge. "The few days we've spent here have included a potential kidnapping and theft, so naturally you guys bonded."

"That's ridiculous." She peeked at Sara from under the wide brim of her straw hat and was perfectly at peace. In spite of the crowds swarming the beach, she and Sara were alone in a magical world defined by sun, surf, and the lazy tug of waves washing over their bare feet, then sucking the sand out from under them. "Are you having fun yet?" she teased.

"You bet, babe. The only way I could have more fun is if I could pull all those clothes off your lovely body and go skinny-dipping."

"Sergeant Aqua would arrest you."

"No, Sergeant Aqua would envy me."

Amanda loved their easy, playful banter. Although it scared her to death, she already knew how she felt about Sara, and if Sara asked, she would hire the moving van tomorrow. But she knew Sara would not ask. Her relationship with Jude had left scorched earth, and only time would tell if love could grow there again.

"Speaking of Sergeant Aqua, you thought she was hot, didn't you, Sara?"

Sara scoffed. "You're the hot one. Why don't you take off your shirt?"

"You know I can't. I'd burn to a crisp." She was wearing her one-piece bathing suit underneath flimsy, soaked cotton pants to cover her legs. "Can we find some shade somewhere?"

"You want me to steal a beach umbrella?"

"If you did that, I'd have to arrest you!" The deep alto voice came from behind, scaring the hell out of them.

"Jesus, Sergeant Aqua, where did you come from?" Amanda almost fainted on the spot, and she prayed the woman hadn't overheard the last part of their conversation.

"Wow, I hardly recognized you without your clothes, I mean without your *uniform*." Even Sara had lost her famous cool as she stared at Aqua in her bikini.

"That's funny. Most people say they don't recognize me without my dog."

It seemed to Amanda that Aqua was staring right back at Sara in *her* bikini. As the bag lady in the middle, she knew which woman's body she preferred, but then, she was prejudiced.

"Speaking of umbrellas, I have one." Aqua pointed down the beach to an oversized rainbow-flag–colored umbrella. "I also have cold drinks and sandwiches, if you'd care to join me."

"Have you been stalking us, Sergeant Aqua?" Sara grinned.

"No, I only stalk bad guys. And if you want to share my lunch, you'll have to call me Paul. Everyone else does."

Sara and Amanda smiled at one another. This was another broad clue. Why was it so many gorgeous lesbians insisted on male nicknames?

"Is it okay if we call you Aqua? By your last name, like in the cop movies?" Amanda was serious. Somehow she didn't see Aqua as a Paul.

"That's cool. I've been called much worse." Aqua smiled.

They agreed to lunch and followed her to her shelter. In the shade, Amanda finally shucked off her outer layers and breathed a sigh of relief. "I don't know why I venture out in daylight. I should only roam the beach at night, like you, Aqua. It appeared you weren't catching any bad guys last night."

"Oh, were you spying on me, Amanda?"

She was surprised the woman remembered her name. "Yes, I was spying. We have a perfect view of the Frisco Fishing Pier, what do you expect?"

"I expect you're right, Amanda. I didn't catch a single bad guy last night, but Tulip got a hit."

"Drugs?" Sara wondered.

"She alerted on an empty paper bag wedged against one of the pier's pilings. The lab just called. It was positive for cocaine. I guess I have to admit my lieutenant was right about pirates."

"Drugs come ashore on boats?" Amanda asked.

"Boats, cars, trucks, and tourist's camera bags—you name it. Sometimes I think the whole island is stoned."

A depressing thought. Amanda, who had never used any kind of drugs other than painkillers for her bullet wound, didn't want to think of the Outer Banks that way.

Aqua continued. "The drugs themselves come from the outside, but the distribution chain is right here, and it's highly organized."

"And the users come from everywhere," Amanda sadly added, thinking about Tammy Tillman. "By the way, our friend remembered the name of the hot-tub guy who came when their wallets were stolen. It was Eddie."

"Last name?"

"Don't know, but he looks like an old-time singer named Eddie Fisher."

Aqua looked blank. Clearly she wasn't into fifties pop stars, so Amanda described him. "Also, he was driving an Island Mer-Maids car."

"That means he works for Lynette Tillman, the mother of Tammy, the girl you're looking for." Aqua frowned. "Putting it in context, I think I do know all these players."

"You have an amazing memory," she noted.

"Not really. It doesn't seem like it in the summer, but in off-season the Outer Banks is like the suburbs of a small town. Everybody knows everybody, or at least you've seen them around. In law enforcement, we tend to cross paths with most of the troublemakers, and Eddie Cutler is one of those."

Aqua paused to finish off a turkey sandwich. "Eddie's been into petty stuff—possession of marijuana and shoplifting cigarettes. He's a follower, not a leader, and if he's working for Mer-Maids, he's likely cleaned up his act. But identity theft is serious business. I'll ask Mike Doyle to follow up on Eddie. We may need to notify the feds."

"What about the Tillmans and Sonny Roach? Are they troublemakers?" Sara asked.

Aqua looked away and began tracing little drawings in the sand. "Well, I know both Lynette and Tammy have had issues with drug addiction, but generally I'd say they were victims. But Sonny?" She roughly obliterated her sand drawing. "I have long suspected he's the cause of those addictions."

"He's a drug dealer?" Amanda asked.

"Can't prove a damn thing, but all those trucks? He has the perfect pipeline for distribution, but most folks around here think the sun shines out his ass. Sonny Boy can do no wrong."

Amanda didn't get it. From the moment she'd laid eyes on the man at Ginny's wedding, she'd pegged him as a lowlife thug. Yet last night at the police station, Deputy Doyle had vouched for Roach. "So does Sonny get a free pass?"

"Maybe it's his male charisma, but I'm definitely immune," Aqua said. "Now, can we change the subject?"

"One more thing," Sara pressed. "You said you know Tammy. Have you seen her lately?"

"Sorry. I know she's your patient and you care about her, but I haven't laid eyes on Tammy for several months. Now, can we change the subject? I have a proposition for you girls…"

Amanda giggled. "How can you proposition anyone when you've been up patrolling all night?"

Aqua also giggled. "Well, there is that. Tulip is home asleep on my bed, and I intend to join her soon. After a night shift, I sleep all afternoon until suppertime, and then I go out and play. And tonight I'd like you and your friends to join me for drinks, dancing, and wild abandon at my partner Jo's restaurant. She's only open to the public Wednesday through Saturday, so tonight we have it all to ourselves…and a few friends."

"Is Tulip invited?" Amanda asked.

"Sorry, only human girls allowed."

# CHAPTER SIXTEEN

*Princess Pam…*

Maya and Shar were up for a party. In all the years they'd been coming to the Outer Banks, they'd never socialized with other lesbians or explored the nightlife. After fretting about what to wear, Shar chose a sparkly low-cut coral tank top that showed off her booty, while Maya was elegant in a flowing, white, ankle-length dashiki that offset her perfect chocolate skin.

"Wow!" Amanda exclaimed when Sara exited their bedroom in a shimmering sleeveless sheath that floated above her shapely knees and perfectly matched her silver-and-gold heels.

"I didn't bring anything dressy," Amanda moaned.

"Don't worry about it, babe. You look fantastic. I'll need to keep an eye on these other women and make sure they don't make a move on you."

*Ridiculous.* As they all piled into Maya's Outback, Amanda felt like an Ellen DeGeneres impersonator in her white pantsuit, starched blue shirt, and classic sneakers. "Do any of you know where we're going? Is it a gay bar, or what?"

Sara laughed. "No way. I know the place. It's just up the street. We could walk there, but we'd get all sweaty. It's a small family restaurant known for its Southern cooking, but since it's off the beaten path, only the locals patronize it. I had no idea the owner was a lesbian."

Maya cut in. "Hate to tell you, Mandy, but we don't have gay bars down here. I've heard about a restaurant up in Nags Head that has a gay bingo night once a month, but other than that—"

"No, that's not quite fair," Shar interrupted. "They have a Pride parade the weekend after Labor Day. It's three whole days of celebration—food, comedy, and music."

Frankly, Amanda didn't care. By nature she was a homebody, and gangs of lesbians made her nervous. She'd stick close to Sara and get through the night, as long as no one asked her to dance. "I wonder if Sergeant Aqua and her partner are out? You'd think that would be hard for a cop."

"Babe, you think it's hard for *anybody* to be out," Sara began, but quickly stopped herself. "But you're right, I think it's probably more difficult for Aqua."

Maya made a right turn into a quiet neighborhood on the Pamlico Sound side. It was an older, mixed-use area with a few unpretentious residences at the end of the street, a twenty-four-hour gas station advertising live bait on the corner, and in the middle of the block, Jo's Family Restaurant. The small painted sign announcing the business was not flashy enough to attract customers, yet the gravel parking lot was full. Amanda wondered if the cars all belonged to Jo's special guests.

They crossed a wide covered porch and entered a traditional seaside bungalow that had been remodeled to accommodate the eatery. Heart-of-pine floors, old mullioned windows, and booths lined the perimeter. Walls had been removed to open up the space, but it looked like two original rooms had been left in place—the kitchen and bathroom, she assumed.

Her senses were on high alert as she noticed two dozen female shapes mingling in the dim interior.

"I love it!" Sara breathed deeply. "It smells like salt and fried chicken, and it feels like someone's home."

"It smells like beer and too many competing perfumes," Amanda grumbled. "Do we have to stay long?" She knew her nerves were showing, but when someone put on a vintage Carole King CD and the women started gyrating to "I Feel the Earth Move," her willies got worse.

"Relax. Try to enjoy it," Sara urged as Paula Aqua sauntered up in a fringed orange shift and cowboy boots, looking nothing like a sheriff's sergeant.

"Welcome, ladies. May I introduce my wife, Jo Baer?" She guided an older woman forward and introduced the four of them.

Amanda was again amazed that Aqua had remembered all their names, but she was mostly captivated by her spouse. Jo was a good fifteen years older than Aqua, her short brown hair streaked with gray, her welcoming smile like a comforting hug. She was small, athletic, and simply dressed in jeans, sandals, and a boldly striped cotton blouse.

"Welcome." Jo shook their hands. "We have chicken tenders, heavy hors d'oeuvres, and plain old peanuts. Plenty to drink— wine, beer, iced tea. Please make yourselves at home. Paula and I will introduce you to the others."

Amanda reached out and impulsively touched Jo's arm. "So you two are *married?*"

Jo nodded. "Yes, we traveled to Washington, D.C., five years ago—as soon as the law allowed. My brother and sister came from Norway to attend."

So that explained Jo's unique, lilting accent. Amanda was entranced. "Congratulations" was all she could think to say.

As Jo headed back toward the kitchen, Maya and Shar made a beeline for the food, and soon they were dancing together in the middle of the room. Although Aqua introduced her to many of the women, Amanda quickly forgot their names. But when Sara dragged her to the dance floor, she forgot to be shy and allowed Sara to lead her in a slow dance, still obsessing about Jo.

"I wonder if lots of Scandinavians immigrate to the Outer Banks. Many are fishermen, right?" she asked, but Sara pulled her closer and mumbled something unintelligible. "I've never known a couple who actually got married. It's amazing, isn't it?"

Sara released her, held her at arm's length, and gazed into her eyes. "So what?"

"Well, it's wonderful, isn't it?"

"It's crazy. I don't understand why we need to imitate straight people. We've always made committed relationships without a certificate to prove we love one another. Who needs it?" Sara walked away toward the bar.

Before she could react to Sara's abrupt mood swing, a tall blonde pulled her into her arms. Amanda was so disoriented, she allowed the stranger to lead her in a bouncy two-step.

"I'm Pam. Who are you?"

Amanda mumbled her name as she tried to remember where she'd seen this woman before. Pam's long, straight, blond hair framed her deeply tanned face, perfect features, and an exquisite throat flowing down to the body of a fashion model. She was the kind of woman who stopped traffic and broke hearts, a movie star. Her ragged designer jean shorts and casual blouse must have cost a fortune.

"Do I know you?" she gasped as Pam spun her around the room and brought them to a stop near the bar.

"I saw you and your partner at the beach, eating lunch with Paula Aqua." When Pam smiled, her sensuous lips parted to dazzling white teeth. "Actually I also saw you two and the other couple last year as well."

She was caught off guard. First, Sara couldn't be classified as her *partner*, and second, Pam had obviously confused her with Jude. "No, you're mistaken. I wasn't here last year. My friend was with someone else then."

Pam regarded her with open curiosity. "So sorry, but never mind. Please come to my table and I'll introduce you."

Before she could protest, Pam captured her hand and led her to a dark corner populated by a half dozen older to elderly women of all shapes and sizes, in attire ranging from suburban conservative to outright flamboyant. As they crossed the space, several other older groupies followed Pam as if she were the Pied Piper.

The odd spectacle jogged Amanda's memory. Yes, she'd seen them all on the beach that morning, gathered around Pam on a colorful blanket. Pam had been serving wine to the adoring group, like the leader of a bizarre, geriatric book club. As she introduced the ladies one by one, Amanda looked for an escape route. And Aqua heroically rescued her, making up some excuse to reunite her with Sara, Maya, and Shar.

"I see you met the princess." Aqua laughed when they were out of earshot.

"What a character. Who is she?" Amanda asked.

"We've never officially met her, but we've definitely seen her around," Maya said. "Who are all those women with her?"

"Those ladies are Princess Pam's uh…how do I say this… clients? Generally she picks them up as lonely strangers on the beach, befriends them, and renders her services."

"What are you talking about?" Sara asked.

Aqua giggled. "Well, depending on the lady's needs, the princess might hold her hand, cook her dinner, pick up her meds, or sleep with her."

"God, are you saying these women pay Pam to sleep with them?" Amanda was appalled. "Isn't that prostitution?"

"They are very loyal clients," Aqua continued with a wicked grin. "Many have regular weekly appointments and no one gets jealous. Pam tells me she used to be a social worker at an old folks' home and volunteered for Hospice. The way she sees it, she better serves the senior community in her new capacity, and it pays much better."

"I love it!" Sara clapped her hands. "As a psychiatrist, I say her method is legitimate therapy and likely more effective than what I can offer talking folks to death."

"You two are unbelievable!" Amanda looked from the law officer to the shrink. Maybe she was an old-fashioned poop, but she thought Pam's profession was just plain icky. "Please excuse me, but I need some fresh air."

As she made her way to the front door, their amused laughter followed her outside. As a rebellious teenager, she used to make that kind of dramatic exit to sneak a cigarette, but this evening she wanted to get as far away from that crazy scene as possible. She needed to clear her head and decide how she felt about all that nonsense. She stomped across the porch, down the steps, and into the parking lot where a full moon cast long bars of shadow across the gravel from the telephone poles across the street. Since there were no security lights or sidewalks, she was grateful for the moonlight as she made her way down the road.

By the time she neared the gas station, she had begun to feel foolish. Why had she rushed out that way? She wasn't usually so judgmental. She wasn't an officer in the sex police. But she couldn't turn back, not until she'd made her point—whatever the hell that was.

Filling her lungs with cool, fishy-smelling air, she batted away mosquitos and walked toward the gas station. As she drew near, she saw a lone female figure leaning against an ancient red soda cooler, which now held doomed minnows. Light from the plate-glass window spilled across the woman's dirty-blond hair and slumped shoulders as she smoked what smelled less like tobacco and more like weed.

Suddenly she looked up and stared at Amanda, sheer terror on her face. Recognition was mutual and instantaneous as they gaped at one another.

"What the hell are you doing here?" Tammy's words broke the frozen tableau. She dropped the joint and ground it under her shoe.

"Tammy, wait!" But she bolted and ran full speed toward Highway 12 and the ocean.

# CHAPTER SEVENTEEN

*Under the dock...*

Amanda ran after her, but Tammy had a good head start. She was younger, fitter, and definitely motivated to escape— although Amanda didn't know why. Her relationship with Tammy had been nothing but cordial, friendly even, as they planned Ginny's wedding cake. But clearly all that had changed, because now she was sprinting like a frightened gazelle.

"Tammy, wait!" she screamed again as the dark figure put more distance between them. Then she realized it was useless to yell, since the wind and the bellow of the surf would drown out her words.

Where was Tammy headed? Obviously she had no car or she would have used it, so whatever her destination, she planned to get there on foot. *Damn it!* After the first surge of adrenaline, Amanda lagged behind. Her wounded side throbbed each time her feet landed. The two glasses of wine she'd consumed at the party burned in the base of her throat, but at least she was wearing her classic black-and-white sneakers.

What if Tammy had no destination? Squinting ahead, she saw her hesitate at the highway, then dart across, dodging traffic. Did she have a death wish? Certainly Amanda did not. As she panted, sucking oxygen into her heaving lungs, she decided the chase was futile, yet she couldn't stop. When her rubber soles suddenly skidded on a patch of loose gravel and her legs flew out from under her, she held out her hands in self-defense and landed knees first, then elbows, then palms-down on the rough ground.

"Jesus Christ in heaven!" In the near-darkness she fingered the legs of her good white pants. They were torn and sticky with blood. Her elbows and hands were bloody too. When tears of anger stung her eyes, however, Amanda was more determined than ever to catch the stupid girl. So she climbed upright and continued the chase.

By the time she reached Highway 12 at the approximate place Tammy had crossed, fate was with her; not a car was in sight. She jogged across, and as her eyes adjusted to the ambient light, she saw a pathway cut through the large dunes looming straight ahead and quickly took it.

Her footing changed abruptly, from the purchase she'd had on the hard surface to the slippery, sinking sand. The extra effort it took to run through that terrain made her injured side scream and her calves cramp as she slogged uphill, grabbing at sea oats to steady herself. The sharp fronds bit into her lacerated hands, yet she kept going.

At the top, she stopped, bent forward, and puked up the wine. When the gagging subsided, she stood up straight and scanned the pulsing horizon. Here the moonlight illuminated the crashing waves and the thin ribbon of beach available at high tide. Looking south, she saw only glittering surf. To the north, the hulking skeleton of the Frisco Fishing Pier loomed below its glowing yellow walls. And just by chance, the Man in the Moon decided to spotlight the bobbing blond head of a fleeing Tammy Tillman as she ducked under the dock.

*Gotcha!* She giggled deliriously. Hoping Tammy was as winded as she was, and that she would pause under the pier to catch her breath, Amanda took her time descending from the crest to the beach. She toppled only once. This time the damage was minimal, thanks to the soft sand landing. She earned a wet butt, though, which made her mad as hell as she strode forward, her soaked panties riding up her crotch.

*Gonna kill her!* she thought with each laborious footfall, but by the time she reached the black forest of the pier pilings, her fury turned to caution. She stopped, stood still and listened. The building above blocked the moonlight, and for perhaps one minute, all she heard was the roar of the waves, like she was inside one of those big conch shells.

Screwing her eyes shut allowed her to detect the undertone of another person breathing. Was it her imagination or was that person whimpering? Or maybe it was two people, because she was sure she heard conversation.

"Tammy?" she called.

Nothing.

"Please, Tammy, I want to help you!"

The next thing she heard was a heavy whoosh of air seconds before the back of her skull exploded in pain. As she fell, she turned her face away from the sea so she wouldn't drown, and then her world went black.

# CHAPTER EIGHTEEN

*Fallen angel…*

"What the hell were you thinking, Mandy?" Sara's face emerged from the circle of faces bobbing above her like helium balloons—three white, one brown.

"I was trying to catch Tammy." Her words were slurred, her mouth dry as cotton.

"So you said when we picked you up from the sand, before you passed out. But why didn't you call us before chasing after her? We would've left the party to help you," said the brown balloon.

"No, we would have stopped you and let Sergeant Aqua handle it." She recognized Shar's voice.

She was lying flat on her back, like a fallen angel. When she dragged her wings upward from her sides like a snow angel, she realized she was lying in the bed she shared with Sara. "How did I get here?"

Sara answered patiently. "Like we told you before, Aqua owns a dune buggy. We got worried when you didn't return to the party, and the attendant at the gas station pointed us in the right direction."

She recalled all the hands lifting her—Sara, Aqua, and someone else—and lying in the backseat, her head in Sara's lap.

"Shar and I didn't know what had happened until Sara called us from Urgent Care. We're so sorry you got hurt, Mandy." This time she recognized the voice as Maya's.

"But where is Tammy? Did she get hurt too?" None of it quite made sense as she looked at her hands and arms covered with bandages. Her aching head was heavy as a tombstone. "Is Tammy at Urgent Care?"

"The doc said your scrapes are superficial, but you'll have one helluva headache tomorrow," Sara said.

Noting that Sara hadn't answered her question about Tammy, she said, "I guess I walked into one of those crossbeams under the pier and hurt myself." But the three of them just looked at one another and didn't comment.

"It's a miracle you didn't drown," Shar said cheerfully. "Aqua took Princess Pam along to help look for you because she knows the beach so well, just like a hooker knows her street corner."

Maya laughed and Sara scowled, while Amanda couldn't quite remember who Princess Pam was.

Sara turned to Maya and Shar. "Would you guys mind leaving now? Mandy needs her sleep."

When they were alone, Sara slipped under the sheet beside her and lay her cool hand on Amanda's tummy, the only part of her that didn't hurt. She turned off the light and their curtain billowed inward with the breeze.

"I'm so sorry, babe. How do you feel?"

She wasn't quite sure, but her brain was fuzzy from some good painkiller. She remembered the feeling from before, when she'd been shot. When she reached out to touch Sara's face, her cheek was wet from tears. "Don't cry. I'm fine. Really. But why won't anyone tell me about Tammy?"

Sara sighed deeply. "I hate to tell you, Mandy, but you didn't walk into a crossbeam. Someone hit you from behind. From the splinters found in your hair, the doctor thinks the attacker used a length of old timber fallen off the dock structure. When we found you, you said Tammy was the only other person you'd seen on the beach, so Sergeant Aqua came to a conclusion. The Dade County sheriff has put out a warrant for Tammy's arrest."

# CHAPTER NINETEEN

*Full fathom five…*

"Why would Tammy want to hurt me?" Amanda asked for the umpteenth time. "Maybe it was someone else? I'm pretty sure I heard other voices. What if they hurt Tammy too?"

She knew she was rambling, grasping at straws, because she couldn't clearly remember what happened under the Frisco pier. She simply refused to believe that the baker who put the little pink guitar on Ginny's cake was violent. But she was grateful that her injuries weren't as severe as they'd seemed last night. In spite of Sara attempting to serve her breakfast in bed, she was already up helping with the dishes.

Sara wouldn't allow her to stick her scraped hands into the hot sudsy water, so she was drying and shelving. After removing her bandages, Amanda proclaimed her scratches were no worse than those earned from a childhood tumble off a bike. Still, everyone babied her.

"Let's call Aqua," Amanda pleaded. "I'd like to tell her myself that I don't think Tammy's to blame."

But Sara was unsympathetic. "Tammy lied to me. She was my patient for six months and never mentioned siblings, a boyfriend, let alone the little detail that she was skipping town and coming to the beach. Who the hell knows what she's really like, or what she's into? Besides, why did she run from you? You've never threatened her in any way."

She had no good answer for that.

"Besides, Aqua already called this morning while you were asleep. It seems our neighbors saw more lights on the beach last night, so Deputy Doyle went to investigate. This happened *before* you got hurt, but he did catch some trespassers."

"Kids smoking pot?"

"Nope, it was an elderly couple from Ohio. They had rented a small motorboat in Nags Head, had engine trouble, and drifted ashore."

"Landlubbers," Shar scoffed. She and Maya had finally started a jigsaw puzzle depicting a row of black cats on a wall. They were grumbling about the difficulty of matching black to black and were even more pissed about the weather. "Why did it have to rain today? Now nobody can enjoy the beach."

"C'mon, cheer up. You know it's gotta happen once in every vacation," Maya said. "We'll go shopping."

"So did the people from Ohio see anything suspicious?"

"Aqua says no. Mike questioned them pretty thoroughly while he helped them tow their disabled boat to a marina in Buxton. They had been using flashlights, so that explains the lights our neighbors saw."

Amanda wasn't confident about Mike Doyle's investigative abilities. Even Sara had called him Baby Face, but she supposed they'd have to take his word for it.

"I do have some good news," Sara said. "I found a Verizon store up in Kitty Hawk, and they have a battery that will work in Tammy's phone. I know it's a long drive, but we'll find great restaurants and shops along the way, so who's up for a rainy-day road trip?"

Everyone raised her hand but Amanda, and then everyone looked at her with sympathy.

"I'm so sorry, Mandy. What was I thinking?" Sara walked up and snuggled her from behind. "How's your head? Do you need something for the pain?"

"No, I'm okay. I just don't feel like riding in the car."

"No problem. We'll stay home and work on a puzzle," Maya said unenthusiastically.

"Absolutely not. You two go and I'll stay with Mandy." Sara kissed Amanda's nape, then tenderly touched the back of her skull where she'd been whacked. The doctor had shaved a small spot about two inches square to accommodate several stitches. "You look like a little duckling."

"Damaged duckling," she whined. In spite of her protestations, she had a wicked headache. The Percocet pills would solve that. She hated Sara's overly protective attitude and despised spoiling everyone else's fun. "Look, I want you all to go without me, really. I'll curl up with a good book and see you at dinner."

"Are you sure, Mandy? Our favorite art gallery is on the way, and we wanted you to see it," Shar said.

"I'm not sure you should be alone." Sara's green eyes betrayed her concern. She tried to draw Amanda closer, but Amanda pulled away.

"Please, give me some space!" she said more harshly than she intended. "I'm a big girl. I'll lock the doors. This is what I want and need." Giving Sara a stern look, she thought, *Maybe Jude let you set the agenda, but I won't.*

Everyone got the message. Sara backed away, while Shar and Maya tried to conceal their glee at escaping the house. After a little more fussing, they all left, promising to return with Chinese takeout sometime around six.

*Thank God.* Amanda breathed a sigh of relief. She took two pain pills, then stepped out on the deck and sheltered under the small overhang. A steady gray drizzle fell on the dunes, and the ocean was half-asleep, the waves licking lazily at the wet sand. Instead of a fresh salty breeze, the humid air smelled fishy and primal. Only a few determined fishermen populated the deserted beach, their cars alone in the otherwise empty parking lot.

Perfect.

Without hesitation, Amanda scampered down to their bedroom. She applied an antibiotic cream to her abrasions, pulled on a pair of loose gauzy pants, a light waterproof jacket, and her sneakers. Her favorite Miami Dolphins ball cap perfectly covered her little bald spot. She slipped her cell phone into her pocket, and then she was ready.

Maybe she was crazy, but she had to see for herself. She wasn't the criminal returning to the scene of the crime, but as the victim, she figured she had the right to investigate, perhaps unearth a clue.

Without wind, the stairs were uncharacteristically solid as she descended the three flights. Instead of its grainy, powdery quality, the sand was mushy as she climbed up and over the dunes. By the time she reached the beach, her head ached, her skin was sore, and her old wound screamed out at her.

*What the hell am I trying to prove?* She walked slowly toward the fishing pier. Everything was so different in the daylight— the low tide exposing a greater expanse of beach, rendering the memory of her attack out of proportion. A lone fisherman glanced at her and waved as she moved into the forest of pilings under the structure. Standing dead center, she rotated three-hundred-sixty degrees but saw nothing out of place—no telltale cigarette butts or shreds of clothing. The tide and rain had long since washed away any footprints. Certainly the board she'd been hit with could be any one of several lying about.

When she looked farther southward, hoping to see the spot where she'd cut through the dunes from Jo's Family Restaurant, the endless curve of shore and seagrass looked all the same— except for one notable difference. Down near the water's edge, she spotted a strange, half-buried object she hadn't seen before. Possibly it had been too dark last night, or perhaps the thing had been concealed by the rising tide.

The sand sucked at her sneakers as she curiously approached the object. The closer she got, the more excited she became, because sure enough, it looked like the edge of a shipwreck from the pirate legends Maya talked about. Forgetting her aches and pains, she picked up her pace and was soon standing above a hull of heavy timber that had once been a seagoing vessel—a very old one.

The gently curving ties were nailed together with thick primitive brads that had almost rusted away. The wood itself was black and covered with barnacles. Had Amanda discovered this amazing relic, or had the islanders known about it forever as it appeared and disappeared with each tide? Was she allowed to touch it?

The wreck was mostly buried, but something that resembled a round metal cistern was visible near the water and she was determined to get a better look. No one was watching, so in spite of the shallow undertow, she got down on her hands and knees to peer inside.

At first it was too dark to see anything, but then, caught up inside the vessel on the ocean side, she saw the fleshy white parts of dead fish. Repulsed, yet curious, she was determined to understand exactly what she was seeing.

The yellow strands floating on the water undulated like seaweed from a stationary point inside. Following the flow, she saw a pale forehead, the bridge of a nose and glassy, staring blue eyes. When she backed away in sheer horror, she dislodged one of the dead woman's arms that had been cocked akimbo. It fell forward palm-up in a bloodless appeal.

Amanda thought she was screaming when she fell back into the sluggish surf, yet no sound came from her mouth. As she gulped air, terror propelled her to crawl crab-like back onto the shore, away from the thing that used to be human. Fearing she would throw up or faint, she sat in the sand, her head down between her knees and rocked gently until the nausea subsided.

*Oh, Tammy, what happened to you?* The mantra repeated in her tortured brain, and she was sure she'd gone completely insane when Ariel's song from Shakespeare's *Tempest* intruded as background music:

*Full fathom five thy father lies*
*Of his bones are coral made*
*Those are pearls that were his eyes.*

# CHAPTER TWENTY

*Yellow tape…*

"That fisherman thought you were dead when he found you curled up on the beach."

Amanda recognized Aqua's voice, and then something cold and wet nudged her under the chin. She lifted her trembling hand and patted Tulip's furry muzzle.

"Poor man was scared to death," Aqua added as she wrapped a light blanket around Amanda's shoulders.

"But I called you on my cell phone, right?"

"No, you called *Sara* and told her what happened. Since she was at the far end of the island, she immediately called me."

"Oh, God!" She gulped as tears flowed down her cheeks. "Is Sara coming?"

"She's on her way." Aqua sat beside her in the wet sand and wrapped a comforting arm around her shoulder, while Tulip lay her head on Amanda's lap and whined sympathetically. Their kindness changed her tears to uncontrollable sobs and suddenly she was shivering. In response, Aqua held her tighter and told her everything would be all right.

How could that possibly be true?

She lost track of time. She closed her eyes, tucked her head between her knees, and allowed Aqua to stroke her trembling back. Had she been a turtle, she would never come out of her shell again. But she couldn't block out the sounds—sirens screaming as more voices crowded the beach, men running and shouting to one another. Gradually the rain subsided and so did her shakes. Hot sun baked her shoulders and Tulip moved away, barking excitedly.

She raised her head and opened her eyes. "What's happening? Who are all these people?"

Now her little patch of beach was enclosed by a flimsy fence of yellow crime tape that flapped as the breeze picked up. The perimeter was large, encircling not only the shipwreck and herself, but a good hundred yards all the way up to the dunes. Beyond that, people were gathering for a closer view of the action.

A half dozen officials stood or knelt at the wreck. Two wore surgical scrubs, masks, gloves, and hairnets as they examined the body. Two wore tan-and-black uniforms like Aqua's, and the last two Amanda recognized as park rangers with their dark gray slacks, light gray short-sleeved shirts, gold badges, and straw hats.

"Everyone gets a little piece of this," Aqua said sadly. "That man waving his arms is my boss, Lieutenant Jason Morgan. The guy with him is from our homicide unit up in Manteo." Aqua explained that the Dare County Sheriff's Office was the civilian law for the islands. They had three district patrol divisions—A, B, and C. Aqua's Division C consisted of herself, Lieutenant Morgan, Deputy Mike Doyle, and a district supervisor. In addition, the sheriff had a narcotics unit and an impact team.

"But here's where it gets complicated," Aqua continued. "Since most of the Outer Banks is part of Cape Hatteras National Seashore, the feds are also involved. The park rangers are theoretically in charge of all the oceanfront up to the dunes, so in that respect, this is their case."

Amanda glanced at the two handsome young rangers—one male, one female—who stood back from the scene, arms folded, giving deference to the sheriff's men. The male looked especially green around the gills as he removed his straw hat and mopped at his pale forehead.

"In practice, our county law enforcement catches most of the violent crimes like burglary or drug-related incidents. And surprisingly, we play well with the rangers in our big ol' sandbox." Aqua smiled.

Amanda was shocked that Aqua was taking this horror in stride, or perhaps she dealt with tragedy by injecting humor. "Do you think she was murdered?"

Aqua stared at Tulip, who was jumping and playing with Lieutenant Morgan. "You know, Tulip really likes my boss. She and Jason bonded when she first arrived from Holland."

"You didn't answer my question, Aqua."

Aqua got picked up a handful of dried sand and let it trickle through her fingers. "I hate to say this, Mandy, but this thing happened very close to where you were attacked last night. Can you remember anything at all beyond what you've told us? Did you see anything?"

As Aqua's implications sank in, she was devastated all over again. "God no! The damned shipwreck wasn't here last night, but I heard voices. I heard someone whimper."

"Male? Female?"

"I just don't know," she moaned.

Aqua sadly shook her head. "I understand. I'm upset, too, because we didn't see anything, either. We drove right by this spot in my dune buggy. At the time we all assumed your injury was an accident and didn't suspect foul play until later. I imagine the body was placed after the tide receded."

*Or before.* But she couldn't voice the thought, because the image of Tammy killed, then trapped and battered all night by the merciless waves was too horrible to imagine.

"Don't worry, we'll get to the bottom of this." Aqua put on a brave face and climbed stiffly to her feet. She brushed off the seat of her black trousers. "How are you feeling, Mandy? Think you can stand up now?" She held out her hand.

Amanda took it and leveraged herself upright. Her skin, her rib, and her head hurt every bit as much as before, but they were the least of her worries. Even her eyes were sore as she looked over at the fishing pier, where folks were coming onto the beach to enjoy the late sunshine. She even saw the lone fisherman, who had apparently found her curled up on the beach. His role had won him a ticket to the inner circle of crime tape, and Deputy Mike Doyle was currently debriefing him.

"Did the fisherman see anything?" she wondered.

"He says not. I understand he's a tourist. I know I've never seen him before."

That made sense. When she took a second look at the extremely tall, thin man with a stylishly trimmed salt-and-pepper beard, designer sunglasses and floppy hat, it appeared his gear was all brand new—from his shiny rod 'n' reel to his rubber boots. One thing was for sure—like her, this guy would never forget his visit to the Outer Banks.

A unique vehicle drove toward them through the sand. It proved to be an ambulance with oversized wheels. She'd seen enough crime TV to know it was coming for the body. Its morbid arrival excited the looky-loos on the perimeter. One woman seemed determined to shove past the yellow tape.

She squinted for a better look. "Oh, it's Sara!" She tugged Aqua's arm. "Please let her through!"

After a few urgent hand signals from Aqua, Sara was permitted access. As she ran across the sand toward Amanda, she almost tripped in her low-heeled shopping sandals. When she pulled them off for an all-out sprint, tears of relief stung Amanda's eyes. As Sara dragged her into her arms, it was all Amanda could do to keep from kissing her.

"Oh, babe, I am so, so sorry!" Soon Sara was weeping too. "Why do these things happen to you?"

Damned if she knew. Suddenly she felt sorry for herself, worse for Tammy, and grieved for the whole fucked-up world. "Why would someone kill Tammy?" she moaned.

Sergeant Aqua poked into their intimate circle and tapped her shoulder. "I don't know how to tell you this, Mandy, but you got it wrong. The dead woman isn't Tammy Tillman. It's her mother, Lynette."

# CHAPTER TWENTY-ONE

*First fight...*

Wednesday morning the sun shone through their curtains. Vacationers' laughing voices could be heard on the beach like nothing had ever happened. They were lying in their nest like spoons in a drawer as noon approached. Amanda knew Sara was awake and had been for some time, but she had given Amanda the healing gift of sleep, hoping it would help them both face a new day.

Eventually Amanda stretched, turned to Sara, and kissed her lips. "It's okay, I'm awake too."

Sara's green eyes popped open and searched hers. She stroked Amanda's back and asked, "How are you feeling?"

Hard question. Her physical pain was minimal, but her emotional state—not so good. "Did Aqua ever say when Lynette Tillman was murdered?"

Sara sighed. "Likely they'll need an autopsy to determine cause and time of death, and even then, they might not release their findings to the public right away."

Amanda turned onto her back and stared at the ceiling, wondering if she would ever get that gruesome image of the watery corpse out of her mind. Last night Maya and Shar had nurtured her with the Chinese takeout they had promised, Sara had administered her meds and tucked her in bed, but no one had been willing to talk about Lynette's death.

"We just met her and her kids Sunday morning, and she's dead by Wednesday. How can that be?" she said. "And Tammy's still missing. What's that about? Sonny obviously lived with Lynette and we know he's violent." Feeling a strange mix of anger and panic, she turned over in bed and took Sara's hands. "I'm scared. What if you and I did something to stir the pot and cause all this?"

"You can't think like that! Our only role was our concern for Tammy. That's what brought us here. Just because we visited her mother—"

"We also visited the sheriff's office—twice," Amanda interrupted. "We expressed our suspicions about Sonny Roach. Then Shar and Maya piled on by suggesting that Lynette's company was engaged in identity theft. We called the cops on them, Sara."

"Yes, and dear Tammy hit you with a timber under the fishing pier. You want me to feel sorry for that crowd?"

"You just proved my point. They're looking to arrest Tammy, and I still don't believe she did it. If that's not stirring the pot, I don't know what is."

Sara pulled free, swung her legs over the side of the bed and sat up. "Let's not argue. I deal with guilt all the time, and most of my patients are carrying the load for the very people who owe them an apology. Don't go there."

"First, I'm not your patient. Second, I'm losing my patience." Amanda jumped out of bed and pulled on her robe so fast it made her dizzy. "Of course I'm upset. What about Lynette's poor children? What will happen to them?"

Sara took a deep breath and walked over to the window. When she opened the curtain, the intense sunlight blinded Amanda. "I'm sorry. Really. I know I sometimes overstep. But look at it this way: her mother is dead and her brother and sister need an adult family member. Those facts should flush Tammy out of the woodwork. Then, if she's innocent, she'll straighten it out with the sheriff."

Without a word, Amanda stomped to the bathroom and locked the door. She sank down on the toilet seat until her dizzy spell passed. *God, we just had our first fight.*

She didn't need a shrink to diagnose Sara's guilt. First, her patient had lied to her, and Sara had been fooled—a blow to her professional confidence. She had brought Tammy into Amanda's life, and now Amanda was hurt. Had their roles been reversed, Amanda would be defensive too. Maybe she should cut her some slack?

# CHAPTER TWENTY-TWO

*Dangerous potential…*

"Lover's quarrel?" Shar asked as Amanda and Sara tromped upstairs like angry storm clouds. She and Maya were seated at the end of the picnic table not occupied by the puzzle, eating leftover Chinese.

"Yesterday was a bitch," Sara answered, as if that explained it all. "Mandy, are you up for breakfast or lunch?"

"Not hungry, thanks, but coffee would be good." Amanda turned to her friends. "Listen, guys, Sara and I are fine. You didn't need to wait for us." She was tired of everyone tiptoeing around her trauma. Yes, she was fragile, but she wouldn't break.

"We weren't waiting for you. We were waiting for this…" Shar held up a FedEx envelope. "My new credit card just came, so now we're hot to trot."

"Congratulations," Sara muttered as the coffee percolated and she put two buttered bagels in the toaster oven.

"But I'm afraid tomorrow will have to be our last full day," Maya announced sheepishly. "I'm so sorry, guys. A problem's come up with one of my court cases, so I have to be back in

Charlotte Friday night, then huddle with my team over the weekend. We should make the best of every minute." She cast a concerned look at Amanda. "Maybe we don't want to go to the beach again, but we should see the lighthouse and the shipwreck museum while we're here."

Amanda was stunned. She thought they would be there until Saturday morning—three more full days, but they'd come in Maya's car and she assumed they'd all have to leave in it. *Shit!* She'd had such high hopes, a sense of romantic adventure, yet she'd accomplished nothing. She was depressed, unreasonably angry with everyone, and plagued by a mission unaccomplished.

"Shar reached into her purse. "The good news is we have a surprise for you, Mandy. We were in the Verizon store when Sara got your SOS, so we left in a hurry, but not before we got the new battery."

She handed her Tammy's cell phone. Its smooth, flat weight burned her fingers with its secret, dangerous potential. "Did you find anything interesting?" she gasped, forgetting to feel sorry for herself.

"We didn't look." Maya grinned. "We figured this is your hornet's nest, so we'd leave it to you to take the first poke."

Three sets of eyes congregated over her shoulder as Amanda plopped down on the couch and swiped the screen. It was much like her own smartphone, with a little green voicemail symbol, which she touched. The mailbox was full with sixteen new messages. Luckily the information was not password-protected.

Sara said, "So check Tammy's outgoing phone calls. You'll see the numbers she called, and they should link to the names in her database."

Sure enough, when she touched the Phone icon, the screen filled with an endless stream of numbers. The last calls were all made the Saturday night after Ginny's wedding.

"Looks like Tammy's been incommunicado since Ginny's wedding," she summarized. "My guess is she fled from Mooresville that very night, accidently leaving her phone behind. Then at some point Sonny trashed her house looking for his money, figured she was headed for the Outer Banks, and then followed her here."

"Right, if you hadn't seen Tammy Monday night on the beach, I'd be really worried," Shar said. "At least you know she's not dead."

"We know she wasn't dead Monday, but today's Wednesday," Sara pointed out gloomily. "Who knows what has happened in the meantime."

But Amanda refused to imagine the worst. As she scrolled through the numbers, she saw that virtually all the most recent calls were made one right after another to a contact identified as *R*.

"She was trying to call her boyfriend, Rusty," she said with certainty. "From the little green arrow pointing inward to the contact, we know they were all outgoing. Not a single blue arrow back to Tammy, so Rusty never called her back."

"Check this out." Maya placed a narrow, perfectly manicured finger on an outgoing call to *Mama*. "She even tried to call Lynette!"

Knowing the hateful relationship between mother and daughter, Sara exclaimed, "God, Tammy must have been desperate!"

In addition to those calls, Tammy had also tried to reach someone named Leo.

"Go to her contacts," Shar yawned. "You can cross-reference the numbers."

She tapped the People icon and brought up Tammy's contacts. Unfortunately the list was very short. R, Mama, Leo, Sonny, and Sara were there, along with several names she didn't recognize. "She didn't have many friends," she sadly concluded.

"Yes, but look, Tammy entered an address for R and it's only a block away," Sara said excitedly. "In fact, check it out, it's on the same street as Jo's Family Restaurant!"

Sara joined her on the couch and snuggled close to speculate, but Maya and Shar soon lost interest and went back to work on the puzzle. As they planned their day, it became clear they intended to revisit the art gallery they'd gone to yesterday and buy a painting they admired.

"You guys should come with us," Maya said.

Amanda ignored her and returned to the phone numbers. "I'm going to call Rusty," she whispered. "I'm sure Tammy is with him."

"Jesus, what the hell will you say?" Sara asked.

"Don't know. I'll wing it." Before her courage deserted her, she touched the *R* number. Her heart pounded wildly as the phone rang.

Someone picked up almost immediately. "Yeah, who is it?" The older woman's voice was raspy from years of cigarette smoking.

She was taken aback. "Is...Is Rusty there?" she stammered.

"Who wants to know?"

"I'm a friend of Tammy's," she answered truthfully and held her breath. One second later, she heard a dial tone. "Whoa, the bitch hung up on me!"

Sara shook her head and gently took her hand. "It seems she's not a Tammy fan. Probably she's Rusty's mother." When Amanda didn't respond, Sara tried again. "Forget it, babe."

"But I can't!" She fought back tears. "I want to go to Rusty's place and see for myself."

Sara was quiet. She leaned over and pressed her forehead to Amanda's, briefly closing her eyes. Then she pulled away and called out to Maya, "Hey, guys, would you mind dropping us off at Jo's restaurant? We'll hang out there while you go to the gallery."

# CHAPTER TWENTY-THREE

*Blackmail…*

By light of day, Heron Way looked different than it had the night of the party. When Shar and Maya dropped them off at the end of the street, Amanda could visually retrace her steps from Jo's place, past the old gas station, and then across the highway to the dunes where she'd chased Tammy. Now the route seemed both shorter and less treacherous.

She pointed to the end of the short street. "Look, one of those houses is Rusty's. And it stands to reason if Tammy was living with him, she could easily have walked down to the gas station for a soda, hung out to smoke, then ran when I spotted her."

"Sounds about right, especially if Rusty's bitchy old mama wouldn't let Tammy smoke in the house."

The parking lot of Jo's Family Restaurant was again filled with cars. She knew the place was open to the public Wednesday through Saturday, so she could be sure the current patrons weren't the gang of lesbians she'd partied with Monday night.

"Jo has lived here awhile," Sara said. "Maybe she knows something about Rusty's family."

"Jo and Aqua live *here*?"

Sara pointed to a long extension that protruded from the back of the restaurant and faced the sound. "She told me the other night that they live back there. I suspect Tulip lives here too."

She looked hard to see the chain-link dog run concealed in the shade of a hidden garden. It made sense to live where you work, as long as you had privacy from the curious customers.

When they entered the restaurant, she was amazed by how bright and airy it was. Clearly it was a favorite hangout for working locals on lunch break and also retirees. Instead of the low conversation and sultry music of the night, today the room was filled with loud chatter and laughter. Several busy waitresses buzzed about, while Jo Baer manned the cash register, hugging her customers with the same winning smile Amanda remembered.

"Over here, girls! Come sit with us." Princess Pam held court in a large, U-shaped corner booth with two of her adoring, gray-haired subjects.

"We were just leaving," the older ladies said graciously as Amanda and Sara approached. They kissed Pam's cheek, and then bustled off to their own pursuits.

"We didn't mean to intrude," Amanda said as she gaped at Pam. By night she had been the femme fatale, seductress extraordinaire. But now she was decked out like a fit and tanned suburban tennis mom. Only the ultra-low cut of her tank top, showing an abundance of cleavage, kept her from looking completely respectable.

Determined not to stare, Amanda slid into the booth with Sara right behind her. "How come you're not out on the beach?"

She sighed dramatically. "Oh, it didn't feel right somehow since that poor woman was murdered only yesterday."

"*Murdered?*" Amanda exclaimed. "Are you sure?"

"Of course she's not sure." Suddenly Jo herself was at their table, an order book in hand. Today she wore jeans, sandals, and a crisp polka-dot blouse. "Paula is the only one with that information, and she wouldn't share at this stage of the investigation."

"C'mon, Jo, I overheard Paul talking to you earlier. It's pretty obvious she was murdered. Paul said it appeared Lynette had overdosed, but the gash on the side of her head said otherwise." Pam scoffed. "Paul questioned Lynette's friends, who swore she wasn't using, so of course they suspect foul play."

Jo gave Pam a sharp kick under the table. "You and your big mouth. I don't know why I put up with you."

"Because I'm your best customer, and I bring all my clients." She grinned and batted her eyelashes.

Amanda looked from one to the other, enjoying the banter between two good friends. It had taken her a moment to remember that *Paula* and *Paul* both referred to Paula Aqua. "When will we know what really happened to Lynette? And what about her kids?"

Jo's pretty forehead creased in a frown. "Paula should know more tonight. She and Lieutenant Morgan are over at Lynette's house now. Far as I know, Tammy is the children's only kin, so she could get custody, if she's willing."

Amanda and Sara glanced at one another, no doubt sharing the same thought. Tammy wouldn't be the most stable guardian, like leaving kittens with Mehitabel the alley cat.

They both ordered a seafood salad, Pam requested more iced tea, and before Jo could rush away, Amanda asked her a question. "Jo, what do you know about your neighbors at the end of the street? A man named Rusty lives there, and we think Tammy Tillman is staying with him."

"No kidding?" Jo's blue eyes expanded. "I've never met Tammy, so I don't know if she's the young woman I've seen around now and then. I definitely don't know anyone named Rusty. We can't see that house too well from here, but the old woman who lives there is hell on roller skates. I've heard her shouting and cursing into the early morning hours. She's an invalid in a wheelchair, so I guess she's unloading on someone."

"So you really don't know them."

"Nope, except occasionally someone drives up in a shiny new dark green Ford F-150 with hunting lights mounted from the bed. He usually stays about an hour, so I assumes he's her caregiver."

"Would Aqua know anything about them?"

"I doubt it. She's seldom here during the day, and we've only owned this restaurant for a few years, so we don't have history with the neighbors."

"Thanks, Jo," Sara said as their hostess hurried away. "I guess this is a dead-end street, literally and figuratively."

"Not necessarily," Pam said. "We could all go visit that old lady after lunch. Maybe I could charm some information out of her?"

"No, only Sara and I will go," Amanda said. "I'm already in up to my armpits, but you're not. Considering the trouble I've attracted so far, you should steer clear."

She was crestfallen. "In that case, I won't tell you what I know about Tammy Tillman and Sonny Roach."

It was blackmail, pure and simple. A waitress brought their food, and after she left, Sara turned to Pam. "What about them?"

"What's in it for me?"

"Would you prefer I tell Jo that once, many years ago, you and Paula Aqua had a thing?"

Princess Pam's eyes narrowed to sharp little sapphires and her full lips compressed to a thin red line.

Sara was relentless. "It's true. I saw you. I was with my friend, Jude, then. I'm sure it was before Aqua and Jo were married, but you and Aqua were an item. It was obvious."

Amanda was incredulous. Considering Aqua's current devotion to Jo, it was hard to imagine her gallivanting with Pam's crowd.

Pam sighed and tossed her long, straight hair. She dropped her voice to a whisper. "Okay, so maybe Sonny is a dealer. He supplies several of my ladies with prescription pain meds. *And* I saw him leaving Lynette Tillman's house early this morning. Soon as he was gone, a young blond woman drove up in a battered gray Toyota. It was like she'd been waiting for him to leave the house. She had a key, let herself in, and a half hour later she came out with two kids—a little boy and a teenage girl. The kids had suitcases. They all piled into the Toyota and left in a hurry."

Amanda and Sara were impressed.

"How did you know we were interested in Tammy and Sonny?" Amanda asked.

Pam lowered her voice. "Paul told me, okay? But listen, you guys, what happened between Paul and me is past history. Over. *Finito.* So please don't tell Jo."

Sara scowled. "Did you tell Aqua what you saw this morning? You sure as hell should have."

"Well of course I did!" Princess Pam put down her iced tea, fished out the lemon, bit down on it and made a sour face. When she had recovered, she took a deep breath. "Jo already told you Paul's over at Lynette's now, and one of the things she'll do is look for a note from Tammy or the kids explaining where they've gone. That's down to me. I told you what I saw. Now are you going to keep my secret?"

"Our lips are sealed," Sara said grudgingly. "And by the way, how did you happen to see Sonny and then Tammy and the kids leaving the house?"

Pam blushed to her bleached roots. "I had a sleepover with one of my ladies last night. She lives in that rich neighborhood fronting the sound. Just so happens the bedroom of her home on Pamlico Club Drive overlooks the Tillman's driveway."

# CHAPTER TWENTY-FOUR

*I'm not buying...*

They paid for their meal, left a generous tip, and then stepped from the air-conditioning into extreme heat. As they acclimated, Amanda said, "You certainly had the goods on Pam. Did you really see them together?"

"Absolutely, but I didn't know who they were back then. You just don't forget two gorgeous women like Aqua and Pam," Sara teased.

"Humph," she snorted as they began walking. She suspected Aqua and Pam had also not forgotten two women as gorgeous as Sara and Jude. "I guess we won't be finding Tammy at Rusty's house now, unless the kids are there too."

"No, but maybe we'll find Rusty and he can answer a few questions."

The house at the end of Heron Way had seen better days. The gravel walkway to the door was overgrown by weeds, pale blue paint peeled from its clapboard walls, and the lower screen in the door had been shredded by the family pet. Before ringing the doorbell, Amanda walked a few paces through the yard so she could peek down the driveway to the garage behind the house.

"I don't see a Ford F-150, but there's a new silver Lexus parked back there."

"Wow, Rusty's mom must do okay," Sara said.

"If she's in a wheelchair, I doubt she drives. Maybe it's Rusty's car?"

Amanda rang the doorbell. As they nervously waited, lightly brushing shoulders for moral support, they first heard frantic yipping, and then rubber wheels rolling across hardwood.

"I'm not buying anything!" The heavy woman who opened the door was flushed, her eyes narrow with suspicion.

"We're not selling anything," Sara responded with a smile.

"Is Rusty home?" Amanda asked as a hairless little rat-like creature bared its teeth and flung itself at the door. "Cute dog. Is it a Chihuahua?"

The hostile woman was slightly mollified by the compliment. "If you're a friend of Rusty's, you'd know he doesn't live here anymore."

She opened the door slightly wider, allowing Amanda tunnel vision through a living room with orange shag carpet to a kitchen tiled with faux green marble linoleum. As she strained for a better look, she saw a long shadow moving on the kitchen floor and realized Rusty's mom was not alone.

"You're that girl who called this morning," she said. "You claimed you were a friend of that skanky Tammy Tillman, so you're not welcome here."

"I'm Tammy's doctor," Sara gently explained. "She's in trouble, and I'm worried about her."

Her bark of laughter brought on a coughing fit. When it subsided, she said, "If you're a doctor, you must be a shrink, 'cause that girl's sick in the head, and trouble is her middle name."

Amanda kept watching as the shadow materialized into a tall man. Her pulse raced as she anticipated the violent Sonny Roach intervening, but as he wandered into the living room to see what all the shouting was about, his build and demeanor was the opposite of Sonny's. He was extremely thin, with a stylishly trimmed salt-and-pepper beard. She almost didn't recognize him without his designer sunglasses, floppy hat, and expensive fishing gear. But when she did, it took her breath away.

"Excuse me, sir!" she called out. "You may not remember me, but I never got a chance to thank you…"

The tall man strode up behind Rusty's mom and kicked the dog away. His malevolent, cold gray eyes looked down at her from either side of a long, patrician nose. "You are mistaken, young lady. I do not know you."

His cold tone sent a shiver down her spine. "I realize I look different now than I did that day when you found me lying on the beach, but—"

"Stop! I have already told you, I have never laid eyes on you."

His command not only stopped her, it caused her to cringe and back up several paces as Sara looked on in bewilderment. Even the Chihuahua whined and took cover in an unseen corner.

Bolstered by her male companion, the old woman placed a heavy hand on the doorjamb. "I think we're done here," she growled and slammed the door in their faces.

For several seconds they were too shocked to move as they listened to the deadbolt snick into place. Sara was the first to recover. She snatched Amanda's hand and literally dragged her down the weeded path. When Maya's burgundy Outback drove up to Jo's Family Restaurant to pick them up, it was all Amanda could do to keep from running.

"What the hell was that all about?" Sara demanded. "Who was that man?"

"He was my fisherman," she gasped. "The one who found me curled up in the sand after I found Lynette's body."

"Are you sure?" Sara stopped in her tracks. "You told me that guy was a tourist, so what was he doing at Rusty's mom's?"

She caught her breath. "I'm sure of two things: something is very wrong, and they were both lying through their teeth."

# CHAPTER TWENTY-FIVE

*The lighthouse…*

Shar and Maya wanted them to choose. "We don't have time for both this afternoon, and tomorrow's our last day. So what now, the Cape Hatteras Lighthouse—or the Graveyard of the Atlantic Museum?"

They chose the lighthouse. As they approached the iconic landmark, a towering white phallus with a wide black band spiraling diagonally upward toward the beacon, Maya explained how the entire lighthouse had to be slowly and laboriously moved inland to keep it from toppling into the Atlantic. Amanda was less interested in the amazing engineering feat and more interested in why her fisherman was at Rusty's mother's.

"I don't get it. The man is so urbane and sophisticated, while Rusty's mom is…" She searched for a kind word. "…is not," she finished as they parked. "He even had a French accent, didn't he, Sara? It just doesn't fit."

Shar laughed as they all climbed from the car. "Use your imagination, Mandy. Maybe the handsome Frenchman was the old lady's lover—the male version of Princess Pam, rendering his services to the straight geriatric population."

Maya punched Shar's arm. "You are such a romantic, my dear. But if you want to hear a *really* romantic love story, let me tell you about the beautiful lady Theodosia Burr, daughter of the famous traitor, Aaron Burr, and her connection to this very lighthouse…"

As Maya lapsed into her zone, waxing eloquent about Theodosia, how she married young Joseph Alston, the first governor of South Carolina, Amanda's mind wandered. As they were swept up in the wave of excited visitors walking through the rustic framework to the park, past the gift shop and restrooms, all she could think about was the encounter with Rusty's mom.

"So Aaron Burr was running for president against Thomas Jefferson, but Alexander Hamilton did everything to thwart Burr and was responsible for bringing about his defeat. This is important because Hamilton was the statesman who arranged for all the lighthouses to be built on the Outer Banks. Indeed, many of the natives still call this one 'Hamilton's Light'."

Half paying attention, Amanda followed them into a large, flat, green lawn of several acres. The freshly mown grass was bisected by a long sidewalk. At one end the majestic lighthouse soared into the cloudless blue sky, while at the far end of the walk, a white wooden farmhouse with a simple covered porch stood at the edge of a scrub forest that surrounded the distant perimeter.

"That must be the lighthouse keeper's residence," Sara said.

As Amanda watched the carefree families playing on the grass, she longed to hold Sara's hand and make the dark mood go away. The death and violence of the past week weighed her down like a heavy coat she couldn't shed.

"Aaron Burr was so angry, he challenged Alexander Hamilton to a duel," Maya continued. "They met on the 'field of honor' in 1804, and Burr shot him dead!"

"Get to the romantic part," Shar prompted.

"Long story short, Burr was arrested for treason when he led an uprising against the United States, but he fled the country for England. His beautiful daughter, Theodosia, who now had a sweet little son named Aaron, was devastated by her father's fall from grace and went completely crazy when baby Aaron died of fever."

"Wait a minute, Maya." Sara stopped them as they all headed toward the tour that was assembling on the lighthouse steps. "So far you've given us a tale of death and insanity. Would you please cut to the happy part?" She cast a concerned look at Amanda.

Maya shrugged. "Well, maybe it's not exactly happy, but it's really spooky. Poor Theodosia was aboard a ship called the *Patriot* when a band of pirates lured it aground with false lights near Nags Head. The pirates slaughtered everyone aboard, except Theodosia.

"The murderous thugs took the crazy beauty to their homes on the Outer Banks and welcomed her to their families. She was passed from house to house until she became an old lady, and still no one knew who she was. One dark and stormy night, Theodosia wandered down to the pounding surf and was never heard from again!" Maya finished triumphantly.

All three women stared at her, waiting for the punch line.

"So…" Maya said dramatically, "today the residents of Nags Head swear that if you walk the beach during the gray season between Christmas and New Year's, you will see Theodosia's spirit strolling alone, looking for her disgraced father and dead little boy."

Everyone sighed.

"Well, that makes it all right, then," Shar scoffed. "So long as all that suffering led to a good ghost story."

A post-and-rail fence surrounded the lighthouse. As her friends got in line, Amanda felt increasingly ill. Her head throbbed and her side seized up. As she looked back across the wide lawn toward the keeper's house, she noticed the families had left the green to join the queue. Then, from the forest, a doe and her fawn crept out into the open, twitching their white-flag tails and sniffing for danger.

She nudged Sara. "Look, it's Theodosia Burr and little Aaron."

Sara glanced at the deer and back at Amanda. "You look pale, babe. Are you okay?"

"Not really. I'd like to sit down somewhere. You three go ahead and enjoy the tour. I saw some benches near the parking lot. I'll meet you there."

"I'll go with you." Sara took possession of her arm.

"No!" She was emphatic. She was so damned tired of everyone, especially Sara, fussing over her. "I'd rather be alone. Please, go have fun." When she turned and fled, she felt Sara's eyes drilling holes in her back, but she didn't care.

She didn't stop until she reached the benches, took a seat, and noticed short rows of granite memorials displayed in the stone plot nearby. Each was engraved with the names and dates of former lighthouse keepers. She hoped they weren't gravestones.

As she pondered this new morbid thought, she gazed out at the full lot, where sun vibrated blindingly off chrome and heat radiated from the pavement. Parked among the empty cars, she noticed one vehicle was occupied. It was idling near the entry, its engine running and windows rolled up. So the passengers could have air-conditioning, she figured.

As she watched, the old gray Toyota backed up and repositioned so it faced the incoming traffic. The maneuver gave Amanda a clear side view of the car and its passengers—a young woman with two children in the backseat. Alarm bells went off as she squinted into the sun. Surely it was Tammy and her kids! The bells in her aching head reminded her of what had happened the last time she chased after Tammy, so she climbed slowly to her feet and proceeded with caution, taking cover behind a tall RV as a new vehicle pulled in.

This new arrival was a shiny, dark green Ford F-150, with a bank of hunting lights mounted behind the cab—precisely the truck Jo had described coming and going from Rusty's mother's house.

*Dear God in heaven!* She took a deep breath and gulped down her fear. The two cars met nose to nose, like they were kissing, then both cut their engines for the rendezvous. A tall redhead jumped down from the truck, and though Amanda couldn't see his face, his body language expressed an urgent need to unite with the slim woman exiting the Toyota.

Eyes hidden behind large sunglasses, her dishwater-blond hair tucked under a ball cap, Tammy was well disguised. Desperate for a better look, Amanda scampered closer, ducking between cars until she was sheltered behind a tour bus. From this vantage point, she recognized the children she'd seen at Lynette's house. The little boy's face was pressed up against the glass, while the bored teenage girl sulked as she played with her cell phone.

Amanda was dying to hear the adults' conversation, which was frantically punctuated by hand gestures and arm movements. When they finally came together in a passionate kiss, she could no longer contain herself. She had a perfect right to confront this woman who had led her on such a dangerous chase.

"Tammy!" she hollered as she strolled up to them. But their embrace continued. Infuriated, she tapped the man's shoulder. "Turn around, Rusty, I'd like a word with you."

Startled, he spun around, his baby-blue eyes wide with shock. But he wasn't half as shocked as Amanda. He was out of uniform in civilian clothes.

"Deputy Doyle!" she gasped. "What are you doing here?"

# CHAPTER TWENTY-SIX

*Into oblivion…*

Amanda was speechless, and so were they, as everyone tried to make sense of the bizarre situation. Her brain raced to the obvious conclusion: from time eternal, redheads had been nicknamed "Rusty," and it was no different for Deputy Mike Doyle. But after all the lies and contradictions, how was it possible that the deputy was Tammy's Rusty?

"I don't understand…" She looked helplessly from one to the other. If anything, they seemed more frightened than she was.

"I can explain, ma'am," Doyle said at last. "I know this looks bad, but Tammy and I are engaged to be married."

Of course, Doyle was the high school sweetheart, the boy Lynette had described as "not worth spit on the sidewalk." She didn't know where to begin, but eventually she found her voice, "You lied to me, Doyle! When Sara and I came to your office looking for Tammy, you acted like you had no idea who she was. And now there's a warrant out for her arrest. Shouldn't you be taking her to jail?"

"Oh, God, I'm so sorry, Mandy!" Tammy wailed. "It's all a big mistake. I never hit you. Why would I do that?"

She was stunned. "So why the hell did you run when you saw me? And if you didn't hit me, who did?"

Tammy wrung her hands and groaned. She yanked off her sunglasses and wiped her red eyes with her sleeve. "I was scared shitless. Don't you get that? I had broken parole, and Sonny Roach was trying to kill me! No one was supposed to know I was on the island, but then you show up, and soon all the world knew."

She didn't follow her reasoning. It wasn't like Amanda had a big megaphone for the express purpose of exposing Tammy. "So why did you hit me?" she pressed.

"I didn't hit you!" she sobbed. "You have to believe me. And I don't know who did. But someone else was under the pier that night. I heard them talking, so I got the hell outta there and didn't look back."

She was somewhat convinced, because she had always maintained that she and Tammy had not been alone that night. She had heard voices, too. At the same time, how had Tammy managed to escape into thin air, when Amanda had been attacked?

She turned to Doyle. "And you believe her?"

"Yes, I do." He pulled up straight and wrapped a protective arm around his fiancée. "She told me how you and Sara tried to help her, hired her to bake your sister's wedding cake, and all. She would never hurt you."

Amanda wanted to believe, and obviously they were both terrified of something, but there were too many inconsistencies. "But you're a sheriff's deputy. Why can't Tammy just turn herself in and clean up this mess? Surely the law will protect her."

"But what about *them*?" Tammy pointed to the children in the car. "While I'm in custody 'cleaning up this mess,' as you put it, Sonny's still free. And I promise you, Mandy, my brother and sister won't be safe in his care."

Amanda wasn't convinced. Sonny Roach was a thug, but surely not a monster who would harm children. She confronted the deputy again. "Look, when we were in your office, you told us Sonny was a harmless badass, and you actually admired his business success, so why the change of heart?"

"That was before Sonny killed my mother!" Tammy cried.

Doyle blushed to his red roots and sweat broke out on his smooth pink cheeks. "I've been wrong about a lot of things, but Sonny was my worst mistake."

"Sonny killed your mother? How do you know? Did you see him do it?" Tammy's accusation floored Amanda. She went weak in the knees as she flashed on the image of Lynette's corpse, her yellow hair floating like seaweed.

"I didn't *see* him do it, but I know!" Tammy wailed. "As God is my witness, Sonny killed Mama, and he'll kill me, too, if he gets the chance."

Amanda's trembling fingers fished the cell phone from her purse. "I'm sorry, but I'm calling Sergeant Aqua. She'll know what to do."

"No, ma'am, I can't let you do that." Suddenly Doyle grabbed her wrist in a vise-like grip. His eyes widened in desperation as he confiscated her phone. "Do I need to toss this in the ocean or can we talk about this?"

The man Sara had called Baby Face currently bore no resemblance to that description. She couldn't tell if Doyle actually meant her harm or if he was simply protecting his beloved, even if it meant risking his job.

While she tried to decide, the teenage girl unfolded herself from the Toyota. "What are you waiting for, Tammy?" she hollered. "Me and Roger are suffocating. Let's go!"

The girl projected the same truculent attitude she remembered from Lynette's, the day the girl called Tammy a whore.

"So where are you going?" she asked Tammy, finally resigned to the fact the little family would indeed leave, no matter how she felt about it.

"It's better if you don't know," Tammy answered.

"She's right, ma'am. It's best you forget you ever saw them."

Noting the firm set of his jaw, and definitely not wanting her phone at the bottom of the Atlantic Ocean, she nodded. She was angry, helpless, and frightened for Tammy. If Sonny was really the killer they described, maybe Doyle was right. Maybe even the sheriff couldn't keep them safe, and the best-case scenario for all involved was for Tammy and the kids to disappear into oblivion.

"Are we good?" Doyle eyed her, arms crossed over his chest as he shuffled nervously from foot to foot.

"At ease, Deputy," she capitulated. "I never saw any of you, all right?"

"Okay." He took Tammy aside, gave her a fat wad of rolled cash, and kissed her one last time. Only when the Toyota had driven out of sight did Doyle climb back into his truck. Frozen to the spot, she waited until he backed up to where she was standing. He tossed her the cell phone. "Please, Miss Rittenhouse. I'm begging you. This is the right thing, believe me."

# CHAPTER TWENTY-SEVEN

*Hot tub…*

Everyone knew something had happened when they finished the lighthouse tour and found Amanda slumped on the bench near the keeper's memorials. Sara took one look at her and said, "Are you sick, babe?"

"I guess I am a little under the weather."

They all assumed it was her head, the old bullet wound, or the accumulation of the week's horrors that had sickened her, and she allowed them to believe just that. For once, she allowed her condition to spoil their fun, because the girls had wanted to take her and Sara out for a celebratory dinner—to make up for the time Amanda had to pay. But she said they'd have to put the restaurant off until tomorrow night, their last night, and that was agreeable to everyone.

So that night Sara hovered while they drank wine, while Shar prepared a homemade dinner of vegetarian chili and cornbread, and Maya entertained them with yet another legend from the Outer Banks. In the meantime, Amanda agonized about whether or not to tell them the truth about her encounter at the lighthouse. A nagging inner voice told her that Tammy and the kids might really be in mortal danger if she spilled the beans.

On the other hand, she was part of an illegal conspiracy. By keeping silent, she was trapped in a bubble of guilt that made it difficult to breathe or speak. By the end of the evening, when they all begged her to get in the hot tub, and even agreed to forgo getting naked in favor of bathing suits if that would convince her to join them, she said yes. But the minute her body hit the pulsing water, the guilt bubble burst and she blurted it out.

"Look, guys, there's something I need to tell you…"

Their mouths hung open in disbelief as they listened. The only sound beyond her voice was the gentle gurgling of the hot tub. When she finished, everyone was speechless for several heartbeats.

Finally, Sara broke the silence. "Jesus, Mandy, you have to call Aqua. This is huge! I don't know what game Deputy Doyle is playing, but he's sworn to uphold the law. He can't keep this under wraps."

"She's right." Maya ran dark fingers through her short Afro. "Now that we know, we're all obstructing justice by keeping it to ourselves. I don't care if Tammy and Doyle are in love. The kids are in danger. If Tammy or Doyle knows something about Lynette's murder, they have to come clean."

"Well, *I* care." Shar placed one hand on her considerable bosom where her heart would be. "If they're engaged to be married, I get it. Even cops get stupid for love. And maybe he's right—Tammy and the kids will be safer if they disappear."

"No, he's dead wrong." Sara was firm. "If you won't call Aqua, Mandy, then I will."

It was a standoff. As she looked from woman to woman, the stubby votive candles ringing the edge of the tub revealed three very different expressions—Sara's jaw was set in determination, Maya's dark eyes rolled with impatience, while Shar seemed deeply worried. All were staring at her.

She figured they had all left their cell phones inside, but when Sara reached over the edge, snagged her shorts, and pulled her phone from a pocket, Amanda's options narrowed. "I don't know Aqua's number," she feebly objected.

"Well, I do." Sara punched her phone icon and the "recently called" list popped up. "We spoke this morning, so all you need to do is touch her number and you're good to go."

She was cornered and bitterly resented Sara putting her there. For the past few days, ever since she'd been attacked under the pier, Sara had been belligerently protective. Amanda had signed up for a lover, not a mother.

"If you insist, I'll go inside and make the call." She didn't need this crew listening over her shoulder.

"No, stay here," Shar said. "You're all wet, and we haven't finished the hot-tub ritual."

"Besides, how will we know if you've told Aqua the truth, the whole truth, and nothing but the truth?" Sara winked.

That wink cinched it. Furious, she snatched Sara's phone, climbed from the tub, wrapped up in her towel, and stomped inside. Moving to the corner of the dark kitchen, where she could still see the deck to be sure no one followed her, she took a deep breath.

Not knowing who was right or who was wrong, or whatever hell might pay, she swallowed her anger and dialed Aqua.

# CHAPTER TWENTY-EIGHT

*The conspiracy theorist…*

They were all laughing and splashing when she returned to the tub. The moon still hung over the ocean, surf still punished the sand, but the votive candles had wilted into sorry little pools. They looked like she felt.

"What's wrong, Mandy?" Sara noticed at once.

"Did you see Blackbeard's ghost?" Maya giggled.

"Yeah, what did Aqua say?" Shar wondered.

She sank onto the wooden bench facing the tub. Shivering, she pulled the towel tighter around her shoulders and hardly knew where to begin.

Sara prompted, "I'm sure Aqua was shocked to hear that Deputy Mike 'Rusty' Doyle and Tammy were lovers, right?"

Maya continued, "And what did she say about Sonny Roach? Did she think he may have killed Lynette Tillman?"

Suddenly she was so very tired. "Yes to all the above, I suppose. Aqua was surprised to hear what I had to tell her, but believe it or not, she has more pressing trouble."

"I don't believe it," Sara said. "What could be more pressing than Doyle's lies or the possibility Sonny is guilty of murder?"

Maya piled on. "I should think Deputy Doyle would be in deep shit. I'm surprised he's not been suspended."

She emitted a small snort of irony. "The thing is, Doyle *has* been suspended. Not because he lied, but because he killed a man tonight."

They stopped splashing and gasped, for once stunned speechless. By then she was so cold she shucked the towel and joined them in the hot water.

"Baby Face killed a man?" Sara was incredulous.

"Sonny Roach, right?" Maya said. "From what you've told us about Sonny, though, I'd have expected it to be the other way around and that Doyle would be dead."

Her teeth chattered. "It wasn't Sonny. It was Eddie Cutler," she managed to say.

"Who?" Shar asked.

"C'mon, Shar, you remember your hot-tub guy, the one who looked like Eddie Fisher? Worked for Island Mer-Maids?" She sank up to her chin in the tub, hoping the heat would drive away the deep chill.

"But why?" Sara demanded. "What happened?"

Determined to get the story right, she explained that after Shar remembered Eddie's name, which connected him to their identity theft, Doyle and Aqua had actually followed through. They had put out a BOLO, "be on the lookout," for the man. Evidently sometime after she had encountered Doyle at the lighthouse, Doyle obtained a warrant to search Cutler's house and confronted him at his front door.

"They got into an argument and Cutler pointed a gun at Doyle," Amanda continued. "During the struggle, Doyle was able to reach his service weapon and got lucky. He says he never meant to kill Eddie."

"Oh, my God!" Shar exclaimed. "What if Eddie *wasn't* the one who stole our wallets? What if I falsely accused him and now he's dead?"

Maya put her arm around Shar. "You can't blame yourself, doll. Of course Eddie did it. Otherwise, why would he pull a gun? It was his guilt that killed him."

"The whole story is bullshit!" Sara interrupted. "Think about it, guys. Rusty Doyle is Tammy's boyfriend. Tammy's mother owns Island Mer-Maids, and Eddie Cutler works for Mama. Are you trying to tell me that Tammy didn't know about Lynette's little side business? Does anyone believe Tammy wouldn't tell her boyfriend?"

"Doctor Sara Orlando, the conspiracy theorist!" Maya teased. "She wasn't always like this, Mandy. Once upon a time, Sara always gave her patients the benefit of the doubt. Next thing you know, she'll be telling us poor Tammy was in on the identity thievery."

"Well, maybe she was." Sara was defensive. "What if everything is connected?"

"If it's connected, Aqua will figure it out," Amanda said.

"What if it's not?" Shar intervened as referee between the prosecutor and the shrink. "In the meantime, poor Deputy Doyle's been suspended, so who's gonna protect Tammy and the kids?"

"It's not like he's been fired or anything," Amanda muttered. "He's just on leave while the department investigates the shooting. Aqua said it appears Doyle acted in the line of duty."

"And now they'll send him to someone like me," Sara added. "To analyze his emotions and determine if he's at risk for long-term depression. Poor little Baby Face."

Amanda was confused by Sara's animosity toward Doyle. Was she reacting to the fact he had threatened Amanda at the lighthouse, or was she simply mad at Tammy for lying during their sessions together and taking it out on the boyfriend? Hurt pride, or overprotectiveness?

"Sara, you need to lighten up," she said. "Think about poor Aqua. She told me they haven't had a homicide on the Outer Banks in years, and now they've had two violent deaths in one week. She was beside herself."

"I hope we didn't bring that bad karma with us," Shar moaned. "But never mind. Tomorrow is our last day. We'll do nothing but have fun—walk on the beach, enjoy dinner at a good restaurant, and then go home—leave it all behind."

Maya lifted an imaginary glass in an imaginary toast. "I'll drink to that!"

Sara did the same.

But Amanda kept her hands under the bubbling water and pinned Sara with her eyes. "Not me. I'm not ready to leave yet, because this isn't over. Sara, can we stay another week?"

# CHAPTER TWENTY-NINE

*A perfect place for spying…*

Amanda had expected more resistance, but when they slid between the sheets, muscles as relaxed as warm jelly from the long soak in the hot tub, Sara said again, "Whatever you want, babe. I'm due more vacation time, so I'll call the office tomorrow and make the arrangements."

Sara hadn't tried to convince Amanda that she needed to get back to welcome Ginny and Trev home from their honeymoon. She hadn't complained that they would need to find new lodgings, since Shar's mother's place was already booked for the following week. Best of all, Sara had dropped the role of overly protective mother and didn't discourage her from pursuing the Tammy mystery.

They made love for the first time in three days, and Sara finally stopped apologizing when she accidently hit one of her cuts or bruises. Instead, they laughed together and changed positions, exactly like Amanda wanted. And when they came at exactly the same moment in a joyous climax of sweet release, she believed they had finally overcome the barriers that had grown between them. Sara had come to realize she wouldn't break.

"We'll have to rent a car." Amanda yawned as they drifted toward sleep.

"Maybe we'll find a sexy little convertible like my Mazda MX-5?"

"In your dreams."

Thursday morning was bittersweet as Maya and Shar rushed to finish their cat jigsaw puzzle. They were upset because Amanda and Sara got to stay, and they were determined to cram all the vacation activities they'd missed into their final day.

"We can't do everything, girls," Sara warned. "And Mandy and I need to use some of the time to find lodgings and rent a car."

"Good luck with that," Shar said gloomily. "It's high season, and you'll find no vacancies."

By the time their friends had finished their healthy granola, and she and Sara had consumed high-cholesterol bacon and eggs, they'd come up with an agenda.

"So we'll do the beach this morning and split after lunch," Maya said, casting a troubled look at Amanda. "We don't have to go anywhere near the fishing pier. We'll choose a beach north of here."

Instead of protesting, she said, "I'd love to explore and see something different."

As it turned out, the skinny strip of wild sand between Buxton and Avon wasn't "something different," but rather more of the same—magnificent unspoiled dunes, endless sparkling waves rinsing over enchanting shell treasures, and a fresh salty breeze that filled her lungs and blew unpleasant thoughts clean out of her mind. It helped that the stretch didn't include an abandoned pier with lethal, head-bashing timber floating about or old shipwrecks concealing dead bodies. And while she saw plenty of happy people, she didn't see Princess Pam entertaining her retinue of elderly lady friends.

Shar grumbled, "I like the beach better in the fall."

Maya laughed. "She's just pissed because she can't take off her top and bare her boobs. Topless beachcombing has become our group tradition in the off-season."

As Amanda visualized Shar's huge tits bobbing unfettered, she decided the sight would seriously distract from enjoying the other natural wonders. "Maybe it's a good thing we came in summer," she mumbled.

When everyone was sufficiently soaked and sunburned, they brushed the sand off and fell into Maya's Subaru in search of lunch. As they drove up and down Highway 12, they noticed all the motels had "No Vacancy" signs and all the restaurants had lines stretching into their parking lots.

"Shit! I don't want to spend our last day standing in line," Shar grumbled.

"Why don't we eat at Jo's restaurant back in Hatteras?" Sara suggested. "I'm sure she'd give us preferential treatment, and she's open to the public today."

"But we've already been there once this trip," Maya whined.

In the end, they agreed a repeat experience was better than wasting precious time, so they turned around and headed south. Along the way, they spotted a car rental place in Salvo. The sign advertised *Topless Vintage Volkswagen Buggies*.

"Check it out, Shar. The cars aren't afraid to go topless, even in summer!" No one laughed at Amanda's lame joke.

But the vintage buggies proved to be too expensive, so while Maya and Shar waited impatiently, Sara and Amanda rented a red Chevy Camaro convertible, which was also not cheap.

Sara nudged Amanda. "Tis not the Mazda, but t'will serve."

"T'will serve very nicely, thank you." Amanda smiled.

They caravanned to Jo's place, and true to Sara's prediction, they went to the head of the line and Joe herself ushered them in. She led them to the same booth they had shared with Pam the day before, but much to Amanda's relief, the princess was nowhere in sight.

"I'm flattered you came back two days in a row." Jo hugged Amanda and Sara with her nurturing smile. "And today I see you've brought your friends. At this rate, I suspect I'll stay in business."

"Judging by this crowd, I'd say business is booming." As she scanned the cheery space, again filled with the laughter of regulars, she realized that Jo and Aqua were likely not plagued by financial worries. "Is Aqua at work?"

Jo rolled her eyes. "Working *overtime*, I'm sorry to say. What with the murder, and now a line-of-duty shooting, the poor thing's hands are full."

"They've confirmed that Lynette's death was a murder?" Amanda jumped on it but Sara jabbed her in the ribs.

"I'm starved. Let's order." Sara effectively ended the topic, while Maya and Shar mournfully explained that today was their last day.

"But Sara and Mandy are staying on another week," Maya finished.

"Only if we can find lodgings," Sara amended. "All the motels are booked up, and we can't find another condo at this late date."

Jo looked thoughtful as she scribbled their orders on her pad. Today she wore a different trademark cotton shirt, this one stenciled with nautical anchors. When she finished writing, she said, "Look, why don't you stay with us? I'd enjoy your company, since Paula's away so many evenings."

Amanda was stunned. "Oh no, we wouldn't want to intrude."

"You would not be intruding. We have large living quarters attached to the restaurant, with a lovely guest bedroom that's always ready—for when my family from Norway comes to visit."

She could hardly contain her excitement, and she could tell Sara felt the same. "You'll have to let us pay the going rate, otherwise we can't accept."

Jo shrugged. "If you insist, but you must let me give you the standard lesbian discount," she whispered.

Everyone laughed as they arranged to move in the following morning. When Jo left to help other customers, Sara clapped her hands with glee but Maya and Shar were green with envy.

"You guys have all the luck," Shar moaned. "Just think of all the interesting women you'll meet here."

Amanda smiled mysteriously. "But the best part is we'll be sharing space with a sergeant close to the murder investigation, and we'll be right down the street from Rusty's mother. Frankly, my dears, it's a perfect place for spying."

# CHAPTER THIRTY

*Died and gone to heaven…*

The postpartum sadness began at their restaurant dinner that night, where Shar finally got a chance to pay. She kept calling it their Last Supper. It continued through breakfast Friday morning, while they did a broom-sweep of the condo and when they packed the cars. Amanda was loading their bags into the Camaro convertible, while Sara and Maya took a final climb up the flights of stairs to be sure no one had left anything behind.

Shar drew Amanda aside. "Mandy, it's been wonderful getting to know you. I'll never forget this vacation, and not just because of all the awful stuff, but because it's been our first with you and Sara."

She snorted. "I'm sure you won't forget it, Shar, but for all the wrong reasons. Since chasing after Tammy was my project, I feel responsible for bringing all the murder and mayhem down on us, and I'm really sorry."

"Don't be." Shar laughed. "It's been kinda exciting, like living in the pages of a suspense novel. No, what I meant was, we really like *you*." She took Amanda into her arms for a big bosomy hug. "I hate it that I said you were just like Jude, because that couldn't be further from the truth. You are completely different from Sara's ex. You are so much nicer and lots more fun."

She was both delighted and embarrassed by Shar's vote of confidence. As the tight hug continued a few seconds too long, she struggled to keep her emotions in check. All she could manage was an incoherent grunt of gratitude when Shar finally released her.

"I mean it, and Maya feels the same. You're the best thing that ever happened to Sara, so don't let her bossiness put you off. For our sakes, I hope she hangs on to you, because we want to do the foursome thing again."

"Thanks, Shar." This time Amanda did the hugging as she fought back tears. "I want that too."

"Hey, break it up!" Sara called playfully as she and Maya joined them. She tossed a pair of sunglasses at Amanda. "You told me you always leave your shades behind, and now I believe you."

Moments later, after another round of hugs, the couples split into their respective vehicles and left the Frisco condo behind. When they reached the highway, Maya turned north and Sara turned south.

Sara exhaled. "I doubt if we'll want to stay at that condo again. Too many bad memories."

"Oh, I suspect those will fade in time." Suddenly she felt shy now that they were alone as a couple. She glanced at Sara. Without the buffer of Maya and Shar and their clowning and hijinks, she wondered how she and Sara would fill the silence. Their relationship was still so new that a week in each other's company could uncover all kinds of quirks that could make or break them. In the past few days they'd hit some roadblocks, but they had endured. "I want to make it work," she blurted. She hadn't intended to say it aloud.

Sara stared at her. "So do I, babe."

In that moment she realized Sara was shy and uncertain too. She took her hand. "We'll be okay."

They had decided to settle in at Jo's before she got busy with the lunch crowd. Knowing how crazy the restaurant had been yesterday, they figured that today it would be a zoo.

As they turned onto Heron Way, Sara said, "I noticed a private driveway before, so we should park back there." The lane was almost hidden. It wound through a grove of pecan trees before terminating at a gravel pad where the black-and-white K9 patrol car was parked. "Looks like Aqua's at home."

"Maybe we should enter through the restaurant," she suggested. "We don't want to surprise them."

They walked through a secret garden planted with hostas, astilbe, Lenten roses, bleeding heart, and other shade dwellers. The dog pen was empty, but Tulip's aluminum water bowl glinted in a patch of sunlight. The residential add-on was a long, low structure sided with natural cedar shakes. French doors opened onto a large patio with a gas grill, comfortable wicker furniture, and a round glass dining table. The corners of the patio included electric tiki torches and outdoor speakers.

"Looks romantic," she sighed.

"Also private," Sara added approvingly. "If we're lucky, Jo will feed us out here."

They left the silence of the garden, followed a path around to the front, and entered the restaurant's dining room. In preparation for the customers who would arrive at noon, the noisy staff was congregated in the kitchen, but Jo was out front wiping down tables and setting silverware.

"Welcome!" she called out to them. "We've been looking forward to your visit." She bustled around behind the bar and brought out a heavy tray filled with new bottles of ketchup and hot sauce. She handed it to Amanda. "Make yourselves useful, girls—a bottle of each on every table."

As they did their chores, Jo followed with napkins and small containers of sugar and sweetener. "Since you're getting the lesbian discount, you may be asked to pitch in from time to time."

"Doesn't Aqua have to bus tables too?" Sara teased.

Jo nodded toward their residence. "She's sleeping. She and Tulip did the night shift, ten p.m. to six a.m. When they got home, Paula was too tired to eat, but Tulip polished off her dog food in three big gulps."

"We can unpack later. We don't want to wake her up," Amanda said. Thinking back, it seemed Aqua's schedule had included a day shift along with this night shift, because she recalled someone saying that she and Lieutenant Morgan were visiting Lynette Tillman's house around noon yesterday. "No wonder Aqua's too tired to eat."

Jo frowned. "Right. You'd think they'd give her a solid day off, but Paula will be back at it in a couple of hours." She loosened the collar of her crisp cotton blouse, this one printed with rows of seashells. "But please don't worry about waking her up, because she sleeps like a log. Here, I'll show you to your room."

The energetic little woman led them through a door in the rear wall. It opened into a sunny passageway that opened into Jo and Aqua's living room. The airy space held a large entertainment center, pastel plaid loveseats facing a stone fireplace, and a big table for eating, playing games, and paying bills. "We use the restaurant's kitchen for our personal cooking," Jo explained, "and that's Paula's office over there." She pointed to an alcove overlooking the garden. It had a small desk with a laptop, a bank of filing cabinets, and a huge puffy dog cushion on the floor.

She glanced at the file folders strewn across Aqua's desk. She imagined peeking through them for classified information about Lynette's murder. The very idea made her blush with guilt.

"This way, girls." Jo ushered them past a closed bedroom door, behind which Aqua and Tulip were undoubtedly sound asleep, and into a second bedroom. "Hope you like it!"

Amanda and Sara gasped at the amazing dream room. The four-poster queen-size bed looked like an antique from a southern plantation, as did the chifferobe for their clothes, the carved dresser, and the Victorian sofa facing a glass wall to the patio. In spite of the rich dark woods, the room was filled with sunshine. A modern, full-size bathroom completed the luxury.

"Like it? We love it!" Sara spoke for both of them.

Amanda was speechless with delight as she imagined crawling under the white chenille bedspread with Sara, maybe even drawing the mosquito netting down around their love nest. "I've died and gone to heaven," she breathed.

"I'm glad you approve." Jo nodded toward the back door. "You can bring your stuff in through there and get settled. Then, if you're hungry for lunch, I have a big pot of Brunswick stew simmering. Come on out for a bowl, on the house."

"Thank you so much!" Amanda said before they both impulsively hugged her. The moment she left, quietly closing the door behind her, Amanda turned to Sara. "What do you think?"

Instead of answering, Sara took her into her arms for a long, lingering kiss. When they finally came up for air, she said, "I think we should accept Jo's offer of a bowl of stew, but then we should take a nap." She cocked her head suggestively toward the bed.

"I agree. Yes to both." Amanda smiled. "But first, are you up for a short walk into the neighborhood? I have an idea…"

# CHAPTER THIRTY-ONE

*The mother lode...*

The twenty-four-hour gas station across the street looked sleepy in the noonday sun. So did the man wearing a wilted green short-sleeved shirt with the moniker *RAY* embroidered on its pocket. Amanda recognized him from the night she chased Tammy. He had been standing behind the counter.

"Are you the owner?" she asked when they entered the store.

"I'm one of them," he answered as he lifted a slice of pizza from a rotating glass warming oven on a stand near the soda cooler. "Want some pizza? It's a good deal—buck a slice."

"No thanks." She studied Ray as Sara wandered toward a display featuring local real estate magazines. He was in his early twenties and would have been handsome but for the pockmarks on his olive skin under a head of silky black hair. She believed he was Pakistani, but second generation, without an accent. "Mind if I ask you a few questions?"

"Talk's cheap. Costs less than pizza." He took a dainty bite and wiped his long fingers on a napkin.

She could only come up with a direct path to where she wanted to go. "Please don't think I'm crazy, but I want to know about the family who lives at the end of this street—older woman in a wheelchair, redheaded son who drives a Ford F-150?"

His eyebrows dipped in a frown. "What's your business with Mrs. Doyle and Mike?"

"Well, it's not exactly about them. It concerns a good friend of mine named Tammy Tillman. Somehow she's mixed up with that family and I think she's in trouble."

"Are you a cop?"

"Not even close." She tried to look worried and helpless so he would trust her, and it wasn't hard because that was exactly how she felt. "Please, Tammy is missing, and the Doyle family is involved."

He took his time and finished his pizza while he continued to watch her through dark, soulful eyes. Trying not to squirm under his scrutiny, she knew she'd found a source. Ray likely saw the Doyles every day, gassed their cars and sold them candy.

"I read the newspapers." He pointed to a stack of *Outer Bank Sentinels*. "Mike Doyle was working on the Lynette Tillman murder before he killed that kid, Eddie Cutler. Are you a reporter, lady, or are you one of the bad guys?"

She looked to Sara for support, but her nose was buried in a magazine. "Listen, Ray, my only concern is Tammy. She's a young, skinny woman with blond hair. She's Mike Doyle's girlfriend. Have you seen her around?"

He lifted a diet Dr Pepper from the case and took a long swallow. "Sure, I've seen Tammy, but not for about a week. She and the old woman hate each other, so Mike doesn't bring her around much anymore. In fact, Mike moved out of the house a couple of years ago and rented a trailer in Salvo so he and Tammy could be together. Seems like a waste of money, though, since Tammy only comes to town once a month."

"Once a month? Really?" Sara suddenly joined the conversation. She came close and leaned seductively against his counter. "You seem to know everything about them."

He laughed and peeked at the cleavage showing at the V of Sara's tank top. "Sure, I'm like the local barber. The regulars tell me everything. Anyone lives here full-time, I can tell you what make and model car they drive."

"Impressive," Sara crooned. "Do you know the tall Frenchman with a new silver Lexus?"

A shadow passed over his face. "I've seen him around, but I sure as hell don't wanna know him. He visits the bitch, Mike's mom, once a week like clockwork. He's in and out in less than an hour, and sometimes he buys gas. Credit card says his name is Troudeaux, but he's never civil enough to say hello. Asshole's cold as ice, and I can't figure why he'd come round a cop's house."

"Why not?" Sara demanded.

He shrugged. "Who knows? But I've seen his kind before. I'd say he's selling."

Amanda and Sara must have looked clueless, because he felt the need to elaborate. "Drugs, you know? Snort it up your nose or shoot it in your arm? Can't be sure, just sayin', you know?"

In spite of the heat, Amanda felt cold as she recalled sitting in the sand near Lynette's body, watching Deputy Doyle debrief her fisherman—a French drug dealer? Obviously Ray's imagination was running away with him. Because the Frenchman had snubbed him and drove an expensive car, he had decided to spread malicious gossip about the man. Still, she would mention all this to Aqua. "Do you know a man named Sonny Roach?"

He pinched the bridge of his nose. "Everyone knows that dude. I don't like to trash my customers, and he buys a shitload of gas for his tow trucks, but he's a bully who likes to throw his weight around. His temper's shorter than his dick, but I gotta say he loves his old lady. Treats her like a queen."

"Lynette Tillman?" Sara asked.

"Yeah, the one who got herself murdered."

Maybe Amanda had hit the mother lode, yet she would take Ray's opinions with a grain of salt. "Did you ever see Sonny with Mr. Troudeaux?"

"God, no! Those two wouldn't exactly run in the same circles. Class versus crass, you know? Who the hell cares?"

When he noticed a buying customer pacing near the cash register, he tore his eyes away from Sara's breasts and walked away to collect some money. Clearly he had tired of the interrogation, but they had already gotten an earful.

"Whoa, can you believe it?" Amanda said when they left the store. "Ray thinks he knows everything about everybody."

"True," Sara agreed. "Just like a shrink, but obviously he's not bound by confidentiality agreements. I don't believe a word he said."

# CHAPTER THIRTY-TWO

*Brunswick stew…*

They were awakened by whining and scratching at their bedroom door. Panicked and disoriented, Amanda quickly untangled from Sara's embrace and tried to figure out where she was. The unwelcome, knee-jerk reaction was borne of years of guilt and suppression, and the fear of being caught in a woman's arms.

From the startled look in her wide green eyes, Sara was plagued by the same fear. But she recovered quicker and touched Amanda's face. "It's okay. We're at Jo's place, remember? We took a nap."

Her murmur of comfort was joined by a more urgent, harsher whisper coming from beyond the door as they recognized Aqua's voice trying to keep Tulip from disturbing them.

"Don't worry, Aqua!" Sara called out. "We're already awake. You can let Tulip in."

Seconds later the big German shepherd padded up to their bed and lay her long nose on the cover. Amanda patted the bed. "You can jump up, girl. We've been formally introduced."

Without hesitation, eighty pounds of dog landed between them and licked her hand. In the meantime, Aqua hovered shyly in the hall.

Sara muttered urgently, "For God's sake don't invite Aqua in until we've put on some clothes."

"Modest, are we?" Amanda giggled, and since it was way too crowded for the three of them, she slid from bed and pulled on her panties, jeans, and a T-shirt. Sara did the same. Tulip stretched out and watched them with interest.

"Are you going to tell Aqua about the gas station guy?" Sara wondered.

She considered. "At the risk of showing off our superior detective skills, I guess we should tell her. After all, it's her case."

"Really? I thought it was yours?"

They had slept much longer than intended. Judging by the dramatic slant of the afternoon shadows stretching across their floor, it seemed quite late. Strapping on her watch, she confirmed it was five p.m.

"Hey, you two!" Aqua called from the hall. "Jo tells me you never had lunch. Why don't I heat up three bowls of her famous Brunswick stew and we can eat together on the patio?"

"Good deal!" Sara licked her lips. "We're ready when you are."

Fifteen minutes later, they were seated at the glass table. Aqua supplied a steaming cauldron of stew, hot buttered rolls, and a bottle of rich red Burgundy.

"I can't drink the wine," Aqua moaned as she ladled out the delicious-smelling meal. "I have to eat and run, I'm afraid. My lieutenant wants the murder, the identity thefts, and Mike Doyle's situation cleared ASAP. But he's too cheap to authorize more overtime to get it done. That's why I'm working short hours tonight—six to midnight—to make up for yesterday."

"Lieutenant Morgan's a tough boss?" Sara inquired.

"Let's just say he's ambitious. He's nearing retirement and he'd like to make captain before he turns in his badge. It'll mean a bigger pension."

As Amanda savored the spicy flavors, she detected pulled pork, chicken, turkey, beef, and lima beans marinated in a vinegar barbeque sauce. But mostly she tasted a dozen questions on her tongue. She had so much to ask Aqua, but so little time.

"We met Ray today, the guy who owns the gas station across the street," she began. "He had a lot to say about Mike Doyle and his mom. Did you know that Doyle lives down at the end of your road?"

Aqua actually blushed. "I'm ashamed to admit that I did not know. Jo says I'm often oblivious to everything but my work. Truth is, I don't pay much attention to the neighbors. I always thought Mike lived in a trailer in Salvo."

"You never saw his big green Ford truck on your street?"

"Hell, I never paid much attention to Mike's truck. He often took his squad car home to use when he did the night shift, then he drove it back to the station the next morning. Guess I'm not much of a detective."

"You also didn't know Doyle had a girlfriend, let alone know that his girlfriend was Tammy," Amanda piled on.

"For Christ sake!" Aqua flared. "Mike doesn't talk about *my* girlfriend, either. We avoid the personal stuff."

She seriously doubted that Aqua's lesbian relationship was a secret in this small town, but she got it. "Ray also knows Tammy, Sonny, and a mysterious Frenchman named Troudeaux," she added in a less confrontational way.

Aqua put down her spoon and frowned at her. "You girls have been busy." Her tone wasn't friendly. "You wanna tell me about it?"

As Sara continued to eat, Amanda realized she was unwilling to contribute, so she plunged in solo. She told Sergeant Aqua everything about Tammy's monthly visits with Doyle, and Troudeaux's weekly visits to Doyle's mom. She shared Ray's view that Sonny was a jerk but that he wouldn't murder Lynette because he loved her, and his theory that the Frenchman was a drug dealer.

"But the weirdest thing, Aqua, is that Mr. Troudeaux is the fisherman who found me on the beach with Lynette's body.

Doyle said the fisherman was a tourist. Either Troudeaux or Doyle is lying."

"Are you finished?" Aqua responded coldly. "First, Ray's a bullshitter. He spreads gossip like horse manure, so he's not the most reliable source. An old lady in a wheelchair and a drug dealer? Are you kidding me? Second, the day you saw that fisherman you were a basket case. I was there, remember? Rather than accuse my deputy of lying, maybe you should consider the possibility that Troudeaux and your fisherman are two different people?"

Aqua's words felt like a slap to her face, and heat crawled up her neck. Yes, the man at Doyle's house had denied being the fisherman, but was she completely crazy? "Look, Aqua, I know what I saw."

Aqua reached into her pocket, pulled out a rubber band, and roughly tied her short black hair into a tight ponytail. Even Tulip, patiently lying under the table, whined at the tension in the air.

"Perhaps you should have an open mind, Aqua." Sara came to Amanda's rescue, her eyes sparking.

During the pregnant silence, Amanda wanted to crawl under the table with Tulip and hide. But after devouring a hot roll, Aqua's temper cooled.

"Look, you're right. I may be an unobservant idiot, but I still can't take the leap that Mike's mom is involved with drugs. I need to think about all this."

"But did Doyle really have to kill Eddie Cutler?" Sara gently pressed. "Did he know his fiancée's mom was implicated in the identity thefts? Was Tammy involved? Would he try to protect her by silencing the man?"

Aqua slowly shook her head. "My instincts say no, because Mike's really torn up about the whole thing. But we are investigating the shooting quite thoroughly. We also have a witness who claimed Mike acted in self-defense, but that witness is a local drunk, so he's not exactly reliable."

"Innocent until proven guilty," Amanda agreed. "What about Sonny Roach?" she asked, hoping that Aqua might share even more.

Instead, she abruptly stood and whistled to Tulip. "Which one of you is Nancy Drew?" She scowled at them. "All I will say on the subject of Roach is that just like his namesake, he's gone into hiding, like a filthy bug under a rock someplace. His buddies at the towing company swear their boss has left town to visit his dying mother in New Orleans."

"How convenient," Sara muttered.

"Have you found Tammy and the kids yet?" Amanda called out as Aqua and Tulip stepped off the patio and headed toward the K-9 unit vehicle in the driveway.

She spun to face them. "Leave it alone, girls, and let us handle it. You'll find a great collection of Wolfe videos in the cabinet. Some of the best gay movies money can buy. I suggest you stay put tonight and sublimate your sleuthing instincts by watching films. Some of them are mysteries. Who knows? Maybe Jo will microwave some popcorn."

She and Tulip got in the patrol car, but before they left, Aqua powered down her window to shout out one last piece of unsolicited advice. "And for God's sake, stay out of trouble!"

# CHAPTER THIRTY-THREE

*Plausible deniability…*

"That went well," Sara said sarcastically as Aqua drove out of sight. "At this rate, they'll toss us out by tomorrow morning."

"Not necessarily." Amanda was thoughtful as she mopped up the last of the yummy stew with the final buttery roll. "Sure, Aqua was pissed because I implied she was an unobservant idiot, but mostly she was mad because she told us too much."

"Obviously Aqua believes Doyle and his mom are innocent of any wrongdoing," Sara said.

"Does she? I detected a flicker of doubt."

Sara took a big gulp of Burgundy and shrugged.

Amanda loved how the red wine glistened on her sensuous lips. It was all she could do to keep from kissing them. She also liked how the deep afternoon light caressed her fair, flawless skin and heightened the blush on her cheeks. *Luscious* was the word that came to mind, like a mango.

"Stop staring!" Sara squirmed under her scrutiny. "Maybe we should cool it."

"Cool what? The seduction or the sleuthing?"

"Not the seduction." Sara grinned. "But we're on vacation. Let's watch the videos."

"Right, but Jo is crazy busy in the restaurant, and Aqua won't be home until midnight, so it's a perfect opportunity…" She smiled mysteriously and let the silence build until Sara was forced to ask.

"Opportunity for what?"

"You don't want to know." She quickly piled their bowls and glasses onto the tray and carried it into their bedroom.

Sara followed. "I don't like this."

She spun around and handed Sara the tray. "You know, if you really want to make up with Aqua, then you should help Jo in the dining room. You told me you put yourself through medical school waiting tables, so why not lend a hand? Jo and Aqua will love you forever."

"What are you up to?" Sara's sunny face darkened with storm clouds.

"Again, you really don't want to know." Ever since they'd arrived that morning, the private files on Aqua's desk had beckoned like a siren's song. She simply had to get a look at them.

"You're not planning to snoop in Aqua's desk, are you?"

"If I don't tell you anything, then you'll have plausible deniability. All you have to do is get busy and keep an eye on Jo. If it looks like she's even thinking about coming into their living quarters, text me and I'll scoot out fast as a bunny."

"That's all?" Sara growled.

"Piece of cake."

"Can I brush my teeth first?"

She knew she had won and thanked her lucky stars. Ever since their spat, after Sara gave up her mother-hen act, she'd given Amanda the space she needed. Yet now she was pushing the envelope and didn't know how long this hiatus would last.

"Thank you, Sara."

After a quick trip to the bathroom, Sara wordlessly picked up the tray of dirty dishes. They walked down the hall to the living room. Sara gave her a last look of pure apprehension and left for the dining room.

Amanda got right to work. She switched on the green-glass library lamp and slid into Aqua's comfortable desk chair. Surprisingly her laptop was in sleep mode, so when she pressed the key, Aqua's screen saver popped up—a beautiful photo of her and Jo on their wedding day. Their radiant faces were open with joy and seemed to say, *we trust you, Mandy*!

Good Lord, already she felt guilty, so she didn't even try to access the computer files. Jo and Aqua had opened their home to them. If she snooped into the laptop, Amanda would literally be biting the hand that just fed her.

The physical file folders, however, felt somehow less sacred. After all, they were just lying around in plain view. But at a quick glance, most of the labels had nothing to do with Tammy. As she let her trembling fingers do the walking, she found an odd tab that bore the initials *L. T.* followed by a cartoon of a skull and crossbones. Naturally she was compelled to open it and discovered a portfolio of newspaper clippings. She also found Aqua's field notes torn from the small spiral book she habitually carried with her, an official-looking background report, and a brief bio of Lynette Tillman. Last, but not least, was a computer printout of the autopsy findings. It had been emailed to Aqua only hours ago from the medical examiner in Raleigh.

Having no shame, she skimmed though the local newspaper accounts of the murder and was shocked to see one with a photo of herself slumped on the beach looking wet and bedraggled. The caption said, "Tourist Finds Body." She groaned.

The background report shed little light on Lynette other than listing minor arrests for drug possession almost a decade ago and several DUIs quite recently. Her bio was even sketchier. It stated that Lynette Parsons had married Leo Tillman in 1985, divorced him in 2009, and that their twenty-four-year union had produced three children: Tammy, Susan, and Roger. It described her profitable Island Mer-Maids business, included a copy of her mortgage and tax records, and not much else. The only useful bit was the name *Leo*, because Amanda recalled he had been one of the few contacts listed in Tammy's phone.

She was almost afraid to read the autopsy report, but when she got into it, much of the medical jargon was above her pay grade. Thankfully no gruesome pictures were attached, or if they had been, Aqua had not printed them out. It wasn't until she got to the final paragraph that Amanda sat up straight and took notice.

Cause of death had been saved for last, like the shocking climax of a good thriller. According to the pathologist, Lynette had died almost instantly from a blow to the temporal lobe of the brain, causing a focal, linear, and rotational concussion that penetrated the brain tissue. The resulting hemorrhaging of the traumatic brain injury caused death somewhere between nine p.m. Monday night and two a.m. Tuesday morning.

By the time the body was found at approximately nine a.m. Tuesday morning, rigor mortis was receding. Livor mortis was present in the subject's breasts and frontal portions of the body in spite of the fact the corpse was found lying on her back, strongly suggesting the body had been moved several hours after death. Information that Lynette had died of an overdose was conspicuously missing, meaning that supposition was only a rumor.

She felt ill, so she skipped the parts detailing the effects of submersion in saltwater to Lynette's poor body, and concentrated on Aqua's field notes stapled to the email. Her chicken scrawl was hard to decipher, but clearly the notes referenced her visit to Lynette's house with Lieutenant Jason Morgan. It seemed Aqua and Morgan had found traces of blood on the corner of a kitchen counter and embedded in the grout between the ceramic floor tiles. Someone had tried to sanitize the scene with ammonia and bleach, but they had detected the blood with a UV black light. They had sent a sample to the lab tech to determine if the blood was indeed Lynette's, but they hadn't yet received an answer.

Amanda's pulse raced as she tried to make sense of Aqua's difficult writing, but one notation was abundantly clear. She'd written *KITCHEN* in large letters, and with a bold arrow pointing to the word, written *LYNETTE DIED HERE!*

*Jesus Christ!* She got her breathing under control and quickly closed the incriminating file. Luckily she'd taken care to remember its exact position on the desk—shoved in between the utility bills and a folder for Jo's Discover Card receipts. Checking her watch, she was amazed to see that less than fifteen minutes had passed since she began snooping. "Thank you, Jesus," she muttered.

For once in her recent past, it seemed she had pulled off a coup without incident, dodged the bullet, or whatever other good cliché described her elation at getting away with this disgraceful act. She stood, stretched, and rolled Aqua's chair back under the desk. Feeling smug, because she was getting the hang of this detective work, she strode purposefully into the dining room, where she spotted Sara calmly and efficiently acting as receptionist.

She walked up to Jo, who was taking money from a long line of satisfied customers. "Hi, how can I help?" She expected she'd be asked to refill the mint bowl or organize menus.

Jo grinned. "It's crazy back in the kitchen. We could sure use another dishwasher."

# CHAPTER THIRTY-FOUR

*Pants on fire…*

They didn't leave Jo's place until late Saturday morning. Once out on the road, they discovered Munchies, a popular lunch place, and the wait for a table was well worth it. Colorful beer posters, funky ocean memorabilia, and aerial photos of the Outer Banks adorned the informal restaurant's rough-hewn walls. Vintage soft rock played while kids of all ages—toddlers to grandparents—laughed and enjoyed their vacations. She wondered why she and Sara couldn't just put away their obsession with the dark side and ease into a real holiday.

But as soon as they were served, Sara brought up Amanda's hijinks of the night before. "I still can't believe you did that, babe."

"Hey, I don't mind washing dishes, but I don't think I'll offer again," she joked, hoping to keep their conversation light.

Sara put down her fish taco and squinted at her. "You know what I mean. I'm sure it's a crime to snoop through a cop's private files."

She put down her crab cake. "You gotta admit I unearthed some pretty interesting stuff. Besides, I didn't get caught."

"Well, that makes it all right, then." Sara frowned as she stole one of her cinnamon sweet potato wedges.

Inevitably they discussed whether or not the ends justified the means. Sara was critical, yet fascinated by the fact Lynette had been murdered in her own kitchen and had lain on the floor until the killer moved her to the beach. They dissected it from every angle. When was the body moved? Had Sonny done it? Had Tammy hated her mother enough to bash her head in? Where were the kids when all this happened? Finally, could one person transport the body without help? The questions were endless and unanswerable.

"If Sonny loved her as much as everyone said, why would he kill her?" Sara absently stole another wedge.

"Maybe it was an accident?" She pulled her basket of sweet potato wedges closer to her side of the table in hopes of enjoying a few herself.

"What are we doing, Sara?" She looked around at the happy faces. "Are we crazy?"

"We are certifiable, and remember, you're talking to a shrink who knows. The only excuse I can think of is our concern for Tammy, but clearly she never asked for, nor does she seem to appreciate our interference."

"You're right, so we should drop the whole thing and have fun?"

"Absolutely." Sara toasted with her iced tea, and they clinked glasses to seal the deal.

On the way out to the car, she lifted her face to the sun and savored the tang of salt in the air. She knew damn well she wouldn't abide by the deal, because the mystery remained unsolved and she intended to follow up on another lead. "I understand there's a marina here in Buxton," she innocently remarked.

"So what?"

"So wouldn't it be fun to stroll around looking at the boats, maybe take some pictures of fishermen and seagulls?"

Sara's expressive eyebrows arched in surprise. "Since when are you interested in the nitty-gritty of the nautical life?"

"Since forever. You'll enjoy something different. Maybe we'll meet some real natives, not just tourists."

Sara reluctantly agreed, but only if Amanda would walk across the highway for what was touted to be "the best ice cream on the island," and then go shopping at the tacky emporium next door that sold souvenirs—starfish to snorkels.

It seemed they were rapidly learning new tidbits about one another. Sara found out Amanda was happiest when she was messing around boats, and Amanda discovered Sara was ice-cream obsessed. She had a charming habit of asking for a free taste of every flavor in the glass case before making her selection of cappuccino with cookies, while Amanda chose plain old raspberry sherbet.

Sara bought her a bright blue T-shirt depicting the Cape Hatteras Lighthouse. "To match your eyes," she said.

So she bought Sara an emerald green T with a flirtatious mermaid. The mermaid's hair was perfectly designed to swirl around Sara's breasts. "To match your boobs," she said.

In the midst of their hilarity, they remembered to ask the clerk where the marina was located. After she finished telling them about the tropical storm that was swirling toward Puerto Rico and would surely hit the Outer Banks, she said, "Turn right at the next street." She pointed north up Highway 12. "Big sign at the dead end says *Skippy's.* You can't miss it."

Sara drove the short block and passed through the open gate in a high wall of chain-link fence. Beyond the gravel parking lot, a deep channel had been dredged in from the ocean. A grid of mooring piers stretched like fingers into the channel, and along each finger expensive sailing and power yachts bobbed gently in their slots.

"Hate to tell you, Mandy, but I don't think you'll catch many working fishermen here. These boats cost bucks deluxe, and likely they're all owned by wealthy out-of-towners."

"But where is everyone? You'd think all these boats would be in use on a perfect first day of August." As she swallowed her disappointment at not finding a more authentic experience, she also looked around for an office. "There's supposed to be a repair shop here."

"How do you know?"

Just then she spotted a prefab Quonset hut. An assortment of outboard motors, rudders, ship's wheels, and other marine parts littered its yard, giving her hope that it was a garage of sorts. At the same time, a large bearded man strode in their direction with a snarl visible in the little oval of mouth not covered by facial hair.

"It's Blackbeard the pirate," Sara whispered with a trace of alarm. "Maybe we're not allowed in here without a membership."

"We'll be okay," Amanda reassured her. "Let me do the talking."

As the burly man got closer, he was not as fearsome as he'd seemed. He was only a kid in his early twenties with big-beard genes, and his high-pitched voice with a Jersey accent definitely spoiled his fierce persona.

"I've never seen you before," he whined. "I know you don't lease a boat slip. Are you here as guests?"

Rather than endure the boy's interrogation, she got right to the point. "Do you know Deputy Mike Doyle?"

"Did I do something wrong? Are you guys like cops?"

"What are you doing?" Sara hissed in her ear.

Undaunted, she continued. "We're following up on an incident from early last week. An elderly couple from Ohio had rented a boat up in Nags Head, but its engine failed and it got washed ashore in Frisco. Deputy Doyle had it towed to this marina to be repaired."

The boy shifted uncomfortably in his size-twelve sneakers. "I don't remember that."

"It happened at night. Was someone else on duty?"

He giggled nervously. "Not hardly, unless you count Boo over there..." He gestured at an ancient black Lab sleeping in the shade of a rowboat upturned on sawhorses. "We lock the gate, and who'd be dumb enough to climb over that bob-wire fence?"

"So how did Deputy Doyle get in?" she pressed.

"How should know, lady? I don't remember a disabled boat, but I'm not the mechanic. Plus I've had a few vacation days recently, so I can't be sure about any of this."

Sara gave her a hard nudge. "Let it go, Mandy. Maybe Doyle had it towed to a different marina."

"Nope, we're the only one fixes boats in these parts." The kid squared his beefy shoulders. "I must have missed that one."

"C'mon, let's go," Sara urged.

But she ignored her. "One more question. Do you know a fisherman named Mr. Troudeaux?"

He laughed like a braying donkey. "I know Troudeaux, but he's no fisherman. That's his boat over there." He pointed to an extremely long, sleek, fiberglass powerboat. Its narrow, iridescent blue and gray hull was designed to be invisible on the water. "It's a cigarette boat. Damn thing has three engines with a combined horsepower of one thousand. Fastest thing on the water, does up to one hundred twenty miles per hour."

"Sounds expensive," Sara muttered.

"You could say that. I heard about one that cost like seven hundred thou."

"Guess you can't buy one of those on a fisherman's income." Even Amanda knew what cigarette boats were used for. "Is Mr. Troudeaux a drug runner?"

He held up both hands. "Now, I didn't say anything like that. Ask me, the guy's just a dick who likes to show off and make a lot of noise. Jeez, when that thing goes all-out, you need earplugs to keep from going deaf."

"So it would be hard to sneak up to shore in a boat like that without someone hearing you?" Sara asked.

"I don't want to talk about this. Like I said, I hardly know the man. He comes around midweek, and then he's gone. He's never once said hello to me."

"So you don't service his boat?"

"No way. He has his own crew. Once he almost pushed a little girl off the dock for touching his stupid boat. Hey, am I in some sort of trouble?"

"Not at all." She smiled sweetly and thanked him. She took Sara's arm and they quickly left the marina.

Before climbing into the driver's seat, Sara stood with her hands on her hips and glared. "You are unbelievable."

"You're right. I'm awesome. I can't say we learned anything new about Doyle, but Troudeaux sure seems suspicious."

"C'mon, Mandy, less than an hour ago you promised you would drop the investigation and we'd both just have fun. Pants on fire! Shame on you."

# CHAPTER THIRTY-FIVE

*Ice cream on the sidewalk…*

Sara didn't stay mad long. By the time they got back to Jo's, they were weak from giggling and singing along with classic rock. They'd put the top down on the snappy red Camaro and cruised the strip, getting most of the lyrics wrong at the top of their lungs and turning more than a few heads. Maybe Sara was supposed to behave like a thoughtful psychiatrist and Amanda like a serious artist, but for one carefree afternoon, it felt so good to let it all hang out. After all, in Cyndi Lauper's immortal words, "girls just wanna have fun."

The restaurant was eerily quiet when they came through the front door. The lights were out, but the tables were set in preparation for the Saturday evening crowd. They sensed that Aqua and Jo were napping.

Quietly letting themselves in, they entered their friends' house and tiptoed past their bedroom. Instead of snoring, they heard soft laughter behind the closed door and glanced knowingly at one another. The thought of Jo and Aqua making love caused a bittersweet knot in the pit of Amanda's stomach.

After many years together, the couple still seemed devoted, and she wondered if she would ever find that kind of lasting happiness.

Sara must have had the same thought, because she quietly took Amanda's hand. "They're good together, aren't they?" she whispered. "What I said about marriage before? I didn't really mean it. If two women really love one another, they should go for it."

Stunned, Amanda was almost afraid to acknowledge the raw need in Sara's eyes. But she squeezed her hand and gently kissed her lips. By the time they reached the privacy of their own room, the intense moment had passed.

"Are you hungry?" Sara's voice was husky with emotion.

She laughed and hugged her. "Are you kidding? After that big lunch, then ice cream, I don't need dinner."

They agreed they'd make do with the chilled wine they'd purchased and order a pizza later, if the spirit moved them. They changed to shorts and their new T-shirts, pushed off their shoes, and settled at the patio table. Amanda chose a chair with a view through the garden to Heron Way beyond.

"Check it out," she said. "I can spy on the Doyles' house from here."

Sara nudged her under the table. "Give it a rest, or I'll make you change places with me."

"Seriously, can we talk about it? What if Doyle's in on it? What if he lied to Aqua about the Ohio couple with the disabled boat? What if he lied to her about the 'fisherman,' or killed Eddie Cutler in cold blood? Don't you think he should be watched?"

Sara took a sip of wine and studied her. "Those are totally wild suppositions, Mandy. What if Doyle's just the nice guy he seems to be? What if the poor guy's sins are the product of your overactive imagination? We've gotten all this information from Aqua, right? And she seems okay with Doyle. Do you think Aqua's lying?"

She was shocked. "Why would *she* lie?"

Sara belted out one of her famous Liberty Bell laughs. "You should see your face. You look like a little girl who just dropped her ice cream on the sidewalk. Of course Aqua wouldn't lie, and she's known Mike Doyle for years. Luckily she didn't hear what you just said, or catch you snooping through her things, or we'd be on our way home for sure."

"But she didn't hear me or catch me, did she? And I still think we're on to something, Sara. Put it all together and a pattern emerges. What if Troudeaux is a drug runner and Doyle's in on it? Since he's a law officer, maybe Troudeaux pays him to look the other way? Maybe Troudeaux visits his mother each week to leave a payoff for her son?"

"Or maybe the Frenchman comes once a week to make kinky love to the lady in a wheelchair?" Sara played footsie under the table with Amanda's bare toes. "Don't you think Aqua's following up on all these theories? Besides, I thought our only concern was Tammy. Where does she fit into all this?"

As Amanda thought about it, tree frogs began their loud buzzing symphony and the sun began to set over Pamlico Sound in the distance. She wondered if this really was the calm before the storm, as the woman in the souvenir emporium had suggested. A scent of gardenia hovered over the patio, reminding her of the corsage she was given for her senior prom. Back in those days, when she was making the effort to date boys, she would never have dreamed that one day in the future she'd be sitting on this romantic patio with her beautiful Sara. She dragged her mind back to the question at hand.

"I don't know where Tammy fits in, but that kid in Mooresville said he saw her with a wad of cash. She gave him some to keep quiet. What if she stole the drug payoff money?"

"From her boyfriend? Why would she do that? Besides, Sonny claimed it was his money, so where does he fit in? For that matter, who killed Lynette?"

Sara's questions were giving her a headache, or maybe she'd drunk too much wine. "I don't know, but I wonder if Tammy and the kids went back to Mooresville to hide out."

"No, Tammy's not in Mooresville." Aqua's voice startled them both. She'd sneaked onto the patio silent as a panther and slid into a chair at their table. "I'd ask for some of your wine, but I'm on duty again tonight."

She wondered how much Aqua had overheard, and prayed—not much. "Hi, Aqua. How do you know Tammy's not in Mooresville?"

She gave them both a hard look. "Well, contrary to what you two might think, the wheels of justice turn slow, but they do turn. One of the first things we did was ask the Mooresville police to check out her house. All the unlucky officer found was an empty house and an unfriendly pit bull named Hamilton."

"Where is she, then?"

"That's a very good question, Mandy, but we're not overly concerned about finding Tammy at this point. In light of your insistence that you heard other voices on the beach the night you were attacked, we no longer consider Tammy your attacker. Why would she? What could be her motive?"

"Well, I was chasing her and she was running. But I've said all along she didn't do it."

"More likely you were bashed by the bad guys we've been chasing lately—drug runners, I suspect," she added begrudgingly. "Since Mike Doyle had already left the beach to help those boaters from Ohio, the shore was wide open for mischief. Besides, now that Raleigh has released Lynette's body, we expect Tammy and the kids will show up at her funeral next Friday."

"Who arranged for the funeral?" Sara spoke up.

Aqua frowned. "Not that it's any of your business, but Sonny Roach provided the money and the instructions."

"I thought he was in New Orleans?" Sara interjected.

"Who's to say he's not?" Aqua scoffed. "Let's just say the check was delivered by one of his towing buddies, no return address or contact information, thank you very much."

Obviously she was upset by her failure to locate Tammy and Sonny, but by her sour expression, she was mainly mad at Amanda and Sara. For one frantic second, Amanda feared that Aqua had discovered her snooping after all. What if she had a hidden surveillance camera installed above her desk?

But then Aqua smiled. "Maybe I should deputize you two?"

"Could you do that?" Amanda stupidly asked.

Her eye roll said it all. "Clearly you haven't taken my advice to butt out, so the best I can hope for is you'll stay out of trouble." With that, she stood up and excused herself. "Tulip is driving poor Jo crazy. She's getting busy with the Saturday night crowd, and I'm the only one allowed to feed my dog. So before I'm considered derelict in my duty, I'd better be on my way."

And then she was gone.

"What do you think?" Amanda asked.

"I think we should order a pizza and watch some lesbian movies."

# CHAPTER THIRTY-SIX

*I pegged him for a sailor...*

At least Jo wasn't mad at them, because the next morning, seconds after they'd dressed, she brought them a hot tray with eggs, sausage, cheesy grits, biscuits, juice, and a whole pot of strong coffee.

"Wow, thanks, Jo!" Amanda said. "Can't you join us for breakfast?"

She looked different today. Instead of a cotton blouse, she wore a loose, low-cut gray string top with sparkly silver sequins in the outline of a gull. Partnered with a gauzy, dove-colored skirt, the outfit flattered her small, compact figure and brought out the silver in her short brown hair.

"Thanks, but no thanks." Jo laughed. "We're closed for the next three days and Paula's off today. So in a few minutes I'll wake her up and we'll go shopping."

"Sounds like fun. I hope she'll take you out to eat so someone else can do the cooking and serving for a change," Sara said.

"That is always part of the plan, my dear."

"What about Tulip?" Amanda wondered.

"You can play with her if you like, but honestly, it's her day off too. Paula's supposed to keep her in her run when they're not working, but since it's so hot, she'll likely leave her snoozing in our bedroom."

"Have a great time!" they called at Jo's retreating back.

They carried the food out to the patio, where Amanda took her regular seat so she could spy on the Doyle's house. She had just taken a sip of her coffee when she heard rustling on the path at the side of the restaurant and suddenly Princess Pam appeared. She was grinning from ear to ear.

"Sorry to butt in, girls, but Jo just told me I'm too late to mooch breakfast off her, so I figured I'd crash your party." She held out an empty cup.

Amanda reluctantly poured her some coffee. "Don't your clients supply breakfast?"

Pam laughed. "I didn't have a sleepover last night, so I'm on my own."

"You can't have my breakfast." Sara yawned. "I'm a little hungover, so I need all the nourishment I can get."

"Me too." She batted Pam's hand away when it reached for her biscuit. "We stayed up late watching movies, so we're sleep-deprived."

Pam wanted to know titles, so they told her they'd seen the classics: *Desert Hearts*, *When Night Is Falling*, and when they were giddy enough, they finished with *Bargirls*.

"Next time call me. I love those films."

Amanda and Sara smiled at one another. Luckily they didn't have enough vacation left to worry about a "next time."

"So have you found Tammy Tillman and her kids yet?" Pam asked.

"No, it seems like we've come to a dead end," Amanda said. "Even Aqua doesn't care about finding her anymore."

"What about relatives? I know her mother's dead, but what about her daddy?"

Suddenly she remembered the name *Leo*. She'd seen it in Lynette's bio the night she snooped and also recalled that contact in Tammy's phone. "It seems her father is alive, but how do we find him?"

"Duh, have you tried the phone book?" Pam asked.

"I already have his phone number," Amanda exclaimed. In less than five minutes, she returned with Tammy's cell phone.

She brought up Leo's number and showed it to Pam, who squinted at it through her amazing sapphire eyes. "It's the wrong area code for the Outer Banks. I have no idea where 305 is."

A bright light flashed in Amanda's brain. "It's Miami. When I lived in Sarasota, I had a friend in Miami and called her once a week. So Leo Tillman lives in Florida?"

"Not necessarily," Sara said. "It only means he lived in Miami when he bought his cell phone. Lots of folks don't bother to change their number when they move, so Leo could be anywhere."

"If you give me the rest of your breakfasts, I'll find him for you," Pam said. "You blackmailed me the other day, so now it's my turn." She snatched Tammy's phone. "Give me ten minutes with this baby and I'll have your answer."

Amanda quickly slid her plate over to Pam, and after one large bite of sausage, Sara did the same. It was clear Pam wanted neither her research efforts nor her eating experience disturbed by their conversation, so Amanda and Sara wandered into the garden while she worked.

"Mandy, do you remember when I told you that Tammy inherited her house in Mooresville from her aunt? That woman's name was Susan Tillman. She must have been Leo's sister."

"Right, and Tammy's sulky teenage sister is named Susan after her aunt, I presume."

Before they could speculate further, Pam called them back to the patio with a victory whoop. "Got it!" she said. "Would you believe Leo Tillman is alive and well and living only an hour from here? As the seagull flies, he's only about twenty minutes away, but we mere mortals need to take a ferry. In other words, Tammy's daddy lives over on Ocracoke Island."

"Are you sure?" On the maps she had studied, Ocracoke looked like a skeletal tailbone that was almost connected to Hatteras Island. She guessed the two had been joined at one time, but now they were separated by a narrow passageway between the Atlantic and Pamlico Sound. According to the brochures she had read, the fabled island was wildly popular with tourists.

"Sure, I'm sure," Pam bragged. "I took the easy way out, girls. I simply called his number. The bad news is no one answered. The good news is there was an answering machine and I heard the message. Not surprisingly—thanks to my unique hookups in this little part of paradise—I recognized the voice."

"How is that possible?" Amanda was astounded.

"That's where my personal expertise comes in..." Pam paused and preened. "As you know, I am intimately acquainted with much of the local senior population. Several years ago I lost the affections of a very special older lady when an old man came courting. She explained that for years, her hubby-to-be had been a captain for hire. He got rich because folks paid him to deliver boats up and down the East Coast—Miami to Maine. Sweet work, if you can get it.

"Can you believe that woman left me for *money*? Anyway, her name was Elyse Kingsley." She paused to remove a biscuit crumb from her cleavage. "Elyse was ridiculously excited when she broke up with me. She said her fiancé intended to settle on Ocracoke, so I'm one hundred percent certain they live there now."

With that, she returned Tammy's cell phone with a flourish. "Now, girls, I think we should catch the next ferry."

# CHAPTER THIRTY-SEVEN

*Hatteras Jack…*

"I feel bad about lying to Pam," Amanda said as they drove into the long line awaiting the ferry.

"Why feel bad? We've been lying to everybody else." Sara laughed. "I just hope we make the next boat, because there are lots of cars ahead of us."

When Pam had suggested they make the crossing together, they had nixed the idea, telling her they already had plans for the day. Pam had been disappointed but understanding, and neither Amanda nor Sara had doubted for one minute she'd hook up with someone else in no time.

"I don't think they'd put us in line unless they had room on the next ferry," Amanda said. At least she hoped this was true, because sitting in the convertible with the top down in the oppressive heat, with no breeze to blow the mosquitos and exhaust fumes away, was not her idea of fun. "Was it crazy to leave for Ocracoke so late in the day? It's almost noon, so we won't have much time on the island before we'll have to turn around and come back."

"Stop worrying. This was something I've been wanting to do with you anyway. Jude and I always made the crossing when we visited the Outer Banks. Ocracoke's a charming place. You'll love it."

This was not entirely reassuring as she imagined Jude the jock, the tennis coach, a woman who never got seasick—unlike her. It had happened only once, when she was six and her parents had allowed her to stuff herself with blueberry pie before taking the ferry from mainland Michigan to Mackinac Island. She'd not taken a ferry since, so maybe she'd outgrown the seasickness—or maybe not.

"What's wrong?" Sara asked.

"Nothing."

All at once the cars began to move, and before she knew what was happening, their Camaro was herded aboard the big ship with all the others. Hood to bumper, they were packed like sardines in a floating, open-air can. She and Sara wound up in what she thought was the stern, but when they began to move, it proved to be the bow.

Sara let out a whoop of excitement as they churned away from Hatteras. "Here's how it works. We can stay in the car during the forty-minute passage, or we can get out and stand against the rail for a great view."

Clearly Sara preferred the second option, so they climbed out and snaked between the parked cars on the starboard side to reach the stern. Along the way, Amanda tested her sea legs—so far, so good. She sensed no rock 'n' roll, only a vibration under her feet from the engine. "I love it!" she said.

"Told you so."

They maneuvered to a chest-high steel wall and propped their elbows on it. From their vantage point, they could watch the road of churning wake the boat left behind, the following seagulls, the receding land, and the occasional ferry bound in the other direction.

"God, I wish Maya was here," Sara said. "This crossing was when she always told the story of Hatteras Jack."

"I'll bite. Who is Hatteras Jack?"

Sara shimmied closer so their hips touched and Amanda could hear her dramatic presentation. "Well, in the year 1790, before sonar and other navigational niceties to keep captains from running aground in these treacherous waters, there appeared a great friend to the sailor—a rare, snow-white albino porpoise named Hatteras Jack. One could say that Jack was a porpoise with a purpose in life…"

Sara's wonderful tale described the ever-changing topography of the sea and inlet bottom—what today might be a deep channel, might next week be a dangerous reef—much to the chagrin of those hundreds who drowned in the Graveyard of the Atlantic. But Jack's self-imposed duty was to lead the ships safely into and out of the Hatteras Inlet.

"Captains of inbound ships would lie off or tack back and forth until high tide. Then they would spot Jack leaping out of the water and swimming in figure eights, his friendly grin smiling from the green waters as he prepared to pilot them ashore.

"With a series of high-pitched squeaks, the piloting would begin, as Jack guided them through the various twists and turns, his white back gleaming just under the surface as he took the boats through the very center of the deep water. Once the escorted ship was safe at rest, the white porpoise would put on a happy show, tail-walking on the waves, a ballet of leaps and flips in the air. He performed swift darts and barrel-rolls just beneath the surface."

Sara's story detailed exploit after exploit for brave Hatteras Jack, until eventually fancy buoys, bells, and horns were put on platforms to mark the channel, and Jack just disappeared.

"Many still speak of him with love and gratitude," she finished. "He was a real Outer Banker in the finest sense of the word."

"You're talking about Hatteras Jack!" A man appeared behind them wearing the official gray uniform and straw hat of the park rangers. "Jack was the best captain who ever navigated these parts, but I need to warn you, ladies, even *he* would have problems if a hurricane hit this coast."

Amanda had noticed the ranger circulating and talking to other passengers, and she'd heard people speculating about the tropical storm moving toward the coast. But one look at the clear blue skies made the idea seem preposterous.

"We're keeping a close eye on this one," he continued. "The National Weather Service is calling her Bella, and by tomorrow we'll know if she flies or fizzles."

"What if she flies?" Amanda asked.

"In that case, you might get stranded on Ocracoke unless you catch the ferry back tonight." He paused to smile at the sky. "Personally I'm not concerned. We've made no plans for an evacuation."

When he moved on to chat with others, Sara said, "I'm not worried. It sounds kinda romantic—stranded in paradise with you."

She wasn't quite sure about that. She'd just finished Pat Conroy's novel, *South of Broad*, about Hurricane Hugo tearing up Charleston, and it was not paradise.

They took turns looking through a viewing machine mounted on the railing, and Sara swore she saw a porpoise playing near the boat. "Check it out, Mandy. It's Hatteras Jack!"

But the second time she put her eyes to the binoculars, the close-up of the rocking waves made her stomach churn. "You know what, Sara, I think I'm going back to the car. I'm tired of standing."

"Are you okay?"

"Sure, I'm fine. You stay and enjoy yourself."

Sara neither argued nor followed as she circled around the port side of the ferry. As she made her way between two rows of cars, reaching out to balance on their fenders, she touched the hot metal of a familiar vehicle. The shiny green Ford F-150 looked just like it had when she had seen it at the lighthouse, only today a single suitcase was neatly stowed in the bed.

She cringed, her seasickness all but forgotten. She had no place to hide. She knew she was hyperventilating, but she had to be sure. Stealing a peek directly through the driver's window, she saw Deputy Mike "Rusty" Doyle. He was sound asleep, his red head rolled back on the seat, his pink cheeks puffing as he snored.

# CHAPTER THIRTY-EIGHT

*On the move...*

"Jesus, Sara, I was scared to death!" Amanda exclaimed. "I was sure his eyes would pop open and he'd see me!"

"Well, he didn't see you, and it's what you wanted, right? You've been sitting in that damn patio chair back at Jo's praying for a sighting, and now we have him where we want him. You know he's here to be with Tammy."

It was one thing to catch sight of Doyle at a distance, but quite another to be trapped on a ferry with him. But Amanda decided the logistics were in their favor. He must have been among the first to board and would leave the ship ahead of them. If he didn't turn around and look at the cars behind him, they might exit unnoticed. Although two women in a red convertible were hard to miss.

"Relax, Mandy, it's perfect. Once we get ashore, we'll just hang back and follow him. He'll lead us right to her."

"Or else I could just call Leo. I have his number right here in Tammy's phone."

"First you didn't want to call Leo, and now you don't want to tail Doyle. What are you trying to tell me, babe? Do you want to forget the whole thing?"

"Maybe I do, but can you put the convertible top up while I think about it? At least that way Doyle won't recognize us immediately if he turns around."

Grumbling, Sara complied. She had just completed the task when the ferry touched land and all the vehicles began disembarking. "You need to make up your mind. Otherwise we'll lose him."

How many moments of truth had she faced during this bizarre vacation? She blew hot, then cold, but so far she'd managed to get beyond her fear. "Oh, for Pete's sake, go ahead and follow him, but please stay several cars back."

Driving away from the ship's landing site, she looked wistfully at the public restrooms, because ever since she'd decided she wasn't going to throw up, she'd realized she badly needed to pee. But they didn't have time. Already Doyle's truck was speeding away from them on the continuation of Highway 12. Indeed, the endless water and dunes on either side of the road were identical to the magical landscape back on Hatteras Island—except for the sky, where some active cumulus clouds were moving in.

"Maybe we'll get some rain," she mumbled.

But Sara wasn't listening. Instead, she pressed the brake and slowed, while up ahead Doyle's truck pulled into a large roadside tavern off on the right. "What should I do?"

"Shit, he's stopping for lunch!" Howard's Pub and Raw Bar was a long, rustic restaurant built up on the usual stilts. It advertised specialty burgers and beers. "Obviously we can't go in, because he'd spot us right away."

"Okay, I'll keep driving and pull off the road a ways up. This is the only route into the village, so we'll catch him again when he's on the move."

She squirmed on her seat. Not only did she need a restroom, she also craved food. It seemed like a decade ago that Princess

Pam had stolen her breakfast on Jo's patio. "I'd kill for a hamburger," she said.

Sara moaned. "Me too, and I hate to tell you, but that place back there has the fattest, juiciest burgers on the planet and fries to die for."

She didn't want to know, and while she was imagining Sara with Jude at that pub, gazing into each other's eyes and chowing down, Sara suddenly pulled off to the right and parked in a lot filled with cars.

"Now where are we?" she sighed.

"You're gonna love this, babe. It's the pony pen. Surely you've heard about these little guys? They're descendants of Spanish Mustangs that have been kept by islanders for centuries. They used to run free, but now they are corralled in a one-hundred-eighty-acre enclosure for tourists to enjoy. C'mon, let's have a look."

Normally she would have jumped at the opportunity, but at the moment she needed to stay put and keep her legs crossed. "You go ahead. I'll stay here and watch for Doyle."

"Okay, holler if you see him." With that, Sara was eagerly off and running, no doubt remembering how much fun she and Jude had feeding the ponies.

As she alternated between checking her watch and watching the highway, she realized she had heard about these mustangs. She'd even seen these ponies in a movie, and now she'd miss seeing them today in person. Darn!

After an excruciating half hour, she screamed for Sara, who came running.

"Did Doyle go by?" She jumped in the car.

"Sorry, no. But can you get me to a bathroom? Fast?"

Sara hit the gas and headed for Ocracoke Village. "I'll zip through town to the public facilities. Then you can pee while I stay on the lookout."

They made it to the Visitor Center just in the nick of time. When Amanda emerged from the restroom, Sara still hadn't spotted Doyle.

"What's the plan?" Sara asked while her stomach growled like a Bengal tiger.

She laughed. It seemed quite possible that they'd missed the green truck, or Doyle had gone elsewhere on the island. She screwed up her courage. "I say we should stop for lunch, but first I will call Leo Tillman."

# CHAPTER THIRTY-NINE

*Leo and Elyse...*

She refused to tell Sara the result of the phone call until they were actually seated in a restaurant eating lunch. They stopped at the first available place, a bar and grill located right on the water at Silver Lake Harbor. SmacNally's also claimed to offer the best burgers on the island, so they both greedily indulged.

"I can't wait. What did he say?" Sara demanded as she daintily wiped a dribble of ketchup off her chin.

"*He* didn't say anything, but the *woman* who answered was very cordial..." Amanda deliberately strung out the suspense as she gazed out at the sparkling blue harbor beyond Anchorage Marina, where clusters of large sailboats, power yachts, and fishing boats gently rocked at their moorings.

"Was the woman Pam's friend, Elyse? Leo's wife?"

"I assume so. She sounded like a lovely person with some sort of a lilting accent—not at all like an old lady." Amanda hadn't felt this relaxed in days as she watched the parade of visitors along the docks feeding seagulls, while pelicans and cormorants went after the fishermen's castoffs. It helped, of course, that she'd been successful. For once her phone call hadn't produced a rude hang-up.

Sara finally reached out and snatched the fork right out of her hand. "I won't let you take another bite until you tell me about the phone call. Was Tammy there or not?"

"Yes, and no." Amanda smiled. "She was there this morning and dropped off the kids, but then she went out for a while. Elyse says Tammy should be back soon, and we're welcome to come over and wait for her."

Sara dropped Amanda's fork. "God, that's wonderful! Do you know where they live?"

"Yep, they live at the end of School Road. It's a wooden house painted dark blue, just past the bookstore."

"That's amazing, babe. You actually found her, and I know exactly where they live."

Amanda beamed. "I think we should tell Aqua."

Sara vigorously shook her head. "What's the big deal? So Tammy's staying with her father. Why would Aqua care?"

Somewhat deflated, Amanda realized the information wasn't exactly headline news. Besides, they'd see Aqua later that evening and tell her that Tammy was okay. "We'd better hurry, though, that sky doesn't look good." Sure enough, in the space of a few minutes, the clouds rolling in looked bruised around the edges.

"The traffic doesn't look good, either." Sara nodded at the bumper-to-bumper jam on Highway 12, most of it headed north to the ferry dock. "We could walk to School Road, or better yet, rent a golf cart."

When she looked at the road, even the golf cart traffic was congested. "Let's walk."

Ocracoke Village had no sidewalks, no stoplights, and was completely unlike what she had expected. As they moved along a sandy berm, passing an odd mixture of beach shanties converted to shops and newer commercial structures, the haphazardness of it all was unique and charming. She saw boat rentals, slushy stands, and a wonderful boutique called The Island Ragpicker, with a gang of cats roaming its parking lot.

"Those are Ocracats," Sara explained. "They kinda live everywhere, and everyone takes care of them."

Eventually they came to School Road, which was little more than a shaded lane, and turned left. It seemed odd to her that these shops were off the beaten path, mixed into residential neighborhoods and all but hidden in thickets of old live oak trees. The bookstore and pottery shop were almost incognito in a garden behind a picket fence. "How do customers find these places?"

"That's part of the fun. It's a treasure hunt."

Leo and Elyse Tillman's place was just as described and perfectly suited a retired sea captain. Ducking under a sagging grape arbor, they picked their way through a sandy, overgrown lawn and climbed up the stairs to a covered porch with well-used rattan furniture and gnarled driftwood displayed as sculpture. An impromptu driveway stretched along the porch, and Tammy's old gray Toyota was parked there.

"Well, she's here," Sara said. "Now that we know she's safe, we should turn around right now and go home."

"No, I need to see her for myself, make sure she's okay." She was prepared to knock on the screen door, when it suddenly opened.

"You must be Amanda and Sara. Did I get that right?" The short, heavy-set African American woman wore a maroon caftan patterned with voluptuous amaryllis blooms and a necklace of carved wooden elephants. Her coal-black skin was lightly sheened with perspiration, and her dark eyes smiled under her close-cropped white hair. "I am Elyse Tillman. Welcome to our home."

In a day full of surprises, Elyse was most astonishing of all. In her wildest dreams, Amanda had never pictured her this way, and it was mind-boggling to imagine her as one of Princess Pam's former clients.

She and Sara stuttered their hellos as Elyse guided them into a small living room cluttered with antique furniture and various exotic objects of art the captain had collected on his travels. The humid space was cooled by a lazily rotating ceiling fan and smelled of incense—or was it marijuana?

"Leo's out in the garage with the kids. They are helping him refinish an old sailboat. I will call him."

Amanda couldn't conceive of Tammy's petulant sister, Susan, sanding or varnishing a boat, but they dutifully followed Elyse onto a shaded deck to see for themselves. Sure enough, as a tall bearded man loped toward them through a grove of pecan trees, she saw both kids hard at work in the garage.

He climbed onto the deck. "I'm Leo. Nice to meet you." He was well over six feet, thin as a telephone pole, with wrinkled skin weathered to a rich mahogany. Only his lively blue eyes, under an unruly mane of blond hair gone to gray, reminded Amanda of Tammy. Yes, she could be this man's daughter.

She shook his hand, which bore the calluses of a lifetime of hard work. Elyse brought out frosted glasses and a pitcher of sweet tea, and they all sat around a battered green metal table. Without going into the disturbing details, they told the elderly couple how they'd come to be friends with Tammy.

Leo fixed Sara with a dark stare. "So you're a psychiatrist. I'm relieved Tammy came to you, because God knows that poor girl needs all the help she can get."

While Elyse nodded in wifely agreement, the garrulous captain began a rant on Tammy's shortcomings, including her attempts to run away from home, her teenage promiscuousness, and her drug use when Sonny Roach came into her life. As they sipped iced tea, somewhat surprised he would share his grievances with total strangers, Amanda sensed something more immediate was disturbing him.

"I'll never know what my ex-wife Lynette saw in that piece of shit, but from that first day when Sonny towed her car to our home, she lost her mind. And it wasn't just the drugs he gave her. They were having an affair while we were married. Did you know that?"

His complexion had darkened to an apoplectic red. Even when Elyse lay her hand on his arm to calm him down, Amanda feared he was working up to a stroke. It wasn't hard to read between his lines and understand why he and Lynette divorced.

"All these years I've sent the kids child support and presents for Christmas and birthdays. And the last one, Roger, isn't even mine!"

Amanda and Sara couldn't suppress twin gasps of surprise at this revelation. No wonder he nursed so much hate in his heart.

At that point, Elyse gently coaxed him to his feet and urged them all to move inside. While it was only nominally cooler in the house, the change of venue did him good. Panting, he sat in a favorite chair and got his breathing under control.

"When my sister died and left her house in Mooresville to Tammy, I was relieved," he said. "She needed to get away from the Outer Banks—and from Sonny. But now that her mother, God rest her soul, has got herself killed, Tammy is back. And that worries me."

Neither Amanda nor Sara wanted to correct him or tell him that Tammy had been coming back long before her mother's death. Instead, Amanda changed the subject. "Do you think the storm will affect us?"

Leo croaked out a laugh. "You bet it will. I can feel it on my skin, and by the pressure in my head. Oh, there's no need to evacuate this time, but the island will flood. If you girls need to get back to Hatteras, you better catch that ferry now, because those sissy captains won't be running tomorrow."

"My husband knows these things," Elyse solemnly added.

"Do you expect Tammy home soon?" Suddenly Sara seemed seriously worried, likely about the weather, and by the way she was fidgeting, she was anxious to be gone.

"Tammy told us she's engaged to be married," Elyse said. "I believe the man who came to take her out must have been her fiancé."

Amanda and Sara exchanged looks. So Doyle had beaten them here after all.

"Perhaps we shouldn't wait for her." Sara was already on her feet. "Please tell Tammy we stopped by, and tell her to call us if she needs anything at all."

"So nice to meet you both, and thanks for the tea," Amanda said as she ran after Sara, who was moving so quickly toward the door, she could barely keep up.

"Please, allow me to walk you out." Elyse followed as fast as her short legs would carry her. Leaving Leo in his chair, she trailed them all the way through the front yard. "I am worried about Tammy," she breathlessly confided. "Her fiancé did not seem like a nice man, and she was definitely not happy to see him."

Amanda stopped. "His name is Mike Doyle. He's a tall redhead with a green truck?"

"Oh, no, miss," Elyse said in what Amanda now recognized as a Jamaican accent. "The man who came for Tammy had big muscles with tattoos, a short blond crew cut, and alligator boots. He was driving a blue van and forced her to get in with him."

# CHAPTER FORTY

*Blackbeard's Lodge…*

After Elyse had gone back into the house, Sara spun to face Amanda. "Why on God's green earth would Tammy go anywhere with Sonny Roach?"

"Maybe he threatened her or her family?"

Again Amanda was hard-pressed to keep up as Sara fast-walked down School Road. "I think he took her against her will."

"I think the whole sorry lot of them are criminals or murderers, and Tammy's in on it." Sara was flushed as she veered right onto Highway 12, heading back toward their car.

"So we abandon her?"

"Wash our hands of her. There's a difference."

A strong wind whipped through Sara's long black hair, and when Silver Harbor came into view, Amanda saw white-capped waves and moored yachts bucking like broncos. "I disagree, Sara. I think Tammy's a victim and she desperately needs our help."

"Do you disagree that we should catch the ferry and get the hell off this island before the storm hits?"

"I agree that would be the sensible thing to do," Amanda coldly replied. She sensed they were on the cusp of their second big fight, and she really didn't want to go there. But to avoid an argument, she'd have to capitulate and leave Tammy to fend for herself. Comparing allegiances, she chose Sara, hands down. "And you're right, Sara, we don't want to miss the ferry, but I hate leaving like this."

As it turned out, they were among the stragglers, the last to desert Ocracoke. Amanda didn't know if the lack of traffic moving toward the dock was good or bad. When they got there, they saw a dozen cars turning back and the ferry was out to sea.

"Jesus Christ, we missed it!" Sara powered down her window and shouted at the man in the ticket booth. "When's the next one?"

He was kind enough to leave his shelter to speak with them. The wind flattened his trousers against his thighs and sent paper scraps skittering across the parking lot at his shoes. "Sorry, ladies, there's no tellin' when the next boat will cross. Could be tomorrow, could be next week. Only Mother Nature knows."

Sara groaned. "We'll never get reservations at a motel."

"No, ma'am, I think you'll get lucky. Judging from all the folks who just left, I expect you'll find vacancies everywhere."

"Thank you, sir," Amanda managed to interject before Sara powered the window back up. Looking at the fury on her face, she didn't know which was worse—Hurricane Bella or Hurricane Sara. "Cheer up, will you? Is it so horrible, hunkering down with me in a romantic motel, riding out the storm together?"

Gradually Sara's death grip on the steering wheel relaxed. After several heartbeats, she laughed. "It sounds wonderful actually. We'll call Jo and tell her we got stranded. Maybe she'll give us a refund if we don't get back this week?"

"Who could ask for more?"

As they headed back into the village, they saw several businesses directly on the water boarding up windows, but the majority of residents didn't seem concerned.

"I wonder if Doyle, Sonny, or Tammy left on that ferry?" Amanda asked.

"If they didn't, it means we're stuck on this island with all three bad guys, and no one from the mainland can get here to rescue us."

"The only person you need to worry about is me." She winked. "Who will rescue you once we get to our motel room?"

Sara pulled up in front of the Harbor Inn. "This is a really nice place. Jude and I used to stay here."

"Then keep moving. I am a completely different experience."

Sara grinned. "Do you want a cottage, bed and breakfast, or a motel?"

"Someplace where we don't need to chitchat and can be completely anonymous. How about that place, Blackbeard's Lodge? The sign says 'B&B atmosphere with hotel privacy.'"

"Jude refused to stay there. She thought the name was tacky."

"Perfect!" The historic wooden structure was yellow with green shutters, white-trimmed decks and porches, and of course, a pirate motif as they entered the lobby. Amanda saw a comfort station with an elderly man sipping coffee from the varnished topside of a repurposed boat.

They approached the receptionist to make reservations. "How long will you be staying?" The man with a crisp white shirt and black bow tie seemed thrilled to have a customer rather than a cancellation.

"Until the next ferry out," Sara grumbled.

The dapper fellow's face fell as he took her credit card and gave them a key to room sixteen.

"By the way," Amanda said, "what happens when there's a medical emergency, or when someone needs to get off the island when the ferry's not running?"

"We have EMS and law enforcement helicopters, ma'am. And some of the rich folks own their own planes. But no one can fly in a hurricane."

She was curious. "You don't by chance have guests registered named Mike Doyle, Tammy Tillman, or Sonny Roach, do you?"

He didn't need to check his register. "No, ma'am, we sure do not."

She ignored Sara's snort of impatience as they moved toward the staircase leading up to their room. But before they took the first step, the man who'd been sipping coffee approached and touched her arm.

"Excuse me, but I couldn't help but hear you ask for Sonny Roach," he said.

Up close the fellow didn't look remotely like a hotel guest in his baggy pants, dirty flannel shirt, and torn sneakers. He also smelled of fried food and sweat, like he hadn't bathed in several days.

"Are you staying here?" Sara asked.

His guttural laugh terminated in a smoker's cough. "Hell no, I'm a moocher. I come round for the free coffee and snacks. They tolerate me, figure I add local color." His shaggy eyebrows dipped in a frown. "I do know the Roach family, though, especially Sonny's brother, Wilbur, and pretty girls like you don't wanna mess with the likes of them."

In spite of Sara tugging at her arm, Amanda was intrigued. "The family lives on Ocracoke? I thought Sonny's mother was in New Orleans."

"Yes, ma'am, his mama might be there, but his daddy and brother lived here for years. The daddy died a few years back. The Roach family home—if you can call a tin-can trailer a home—is up on North Pond Road, at the very end. Sits right on the water of the Sound. Will and me are friends, you could say. He digs up night crawlers and seines minnows, and I sell his bait. If his no-good brother's on the island, he'll be stayin' with Will."

"Oh, thank you so much!" Amanda felt like she'd hit the jackpot. Had she not feared it would offend him, she'd pass the old guy a ten. Instead, she watched him walk back to the hospitality station for more freebies.

"Did you hear that, Sara? Now we know where to find Tammy. We know damn well she's in terrible trouble. Even this guy who knows them well warned us about the Roach family. We have to go check on her."

# CHAPTER FORTY-ONE

*The dark woods…*

Ignoring Amanda's plea, Sara stomped upstairs to their room, and of course, Amanda had to follow. The space was homey and welcoming, with traditional furniture, a nautical motif, and a modern bathroom. One look at the queen-sized, four-poster bed, and Amanda wished like hell she didn't have to go anywhere.

Sara grumbled, "Sure you want to venture out?"

"Tammy needs us. We have to visit that trailer and see if Sonny's van is there. If it's not, then we'll come right back," she said as firmly as possible, without outright insisting.

"Oh Jesus Christ!" Sara cursed, but then sighed in resignation. "It seems we have to do it your way, but first I'm calling Jo to let her know what's happening."

Amanda rushed into the bathroom and washed her face while Sara made the call. When she returned, Sara was sitting on the bed and didn't look happy. "Aqua picked up instead of Jo. When I explained what we were up to, she went ballistic. I didn't know the woman was even capable of such foul language."

"Just because we got stranded on Ocracoke?"

"I told her the truth. She made me promise we'd go nowhere near Sonny, or she would personally commandeer the sheriff's helicopter and drag us back to Hatteras."

"What did she say about Sonny possibly kidnapping Tammy?"

"She said we should absolutely steer clear of them. Besides, I think by now Tammy's probably safely home at Leo's."

"Wanna bet?" She took out Tammy's cell phone and called the sea captain. She listened to Elyse's frantic response, hung up, and said, "She's not home, and Leo is panicking."

"Then let Leo drive over to North Pond Road."

"They don't own a car."

Ten minutes later, in spite of Sara's protests and the dapper desk clerk's warning to return to Blackbeard's Lodge posthaste, because the hotel was preparing to "batten down the hatches," they were on the move. They drove north and made a right on British Cemetery Road. By then leaf debris and small branches were skidding across their path and a few stray droplets dotted the windshield.

"Is that really a British cemetery?" Amanda saw gravestones behind a white picket fence.

"According to Maya, a British trawler was torpedoed by a German submarine during World War Two. Four sailors drowned and washed ashore. The locals buried them, and every year Queen Elizabeth sends a new British flag to honor them."

Perhaps it was because of the gloomy day, but the story depressed her as they turned left on Pamlico Shores, then right on North Pond. "If the man was correct, then the Roach trailer should be at the end of this street."

The road ended and a light rain began. Sara pulled onto a gravel pad surrounded by a scrub cedar forest and turned off the engine. As they peered into the dark woods, they saw no sign of life, let alone a trailer.

"The old guy was wrong. Let's go—"

"Wait, Sara!" Amanda saw movement between the trees, and suddenly a tall young man came loping toward their car.

"You girls lookin' for me?" He rapped on the window.

The family resemblance was striking, yet the two brothers couldn't have been more different. Assuming this was Wilbur Roach, he lacked Sonny's muscular physique and intimidating attitude. He had the same blond hair, but Will's was long and greasy, not crew cut. His blue eyes were identical, but instead of Sonny's malevolent focus, they were oddly blank.

"I just dug me some fresh night crawlers." His smile exposed a row of unfortunate teeth. "They say the fish bite best before a storm."

She returned the smile. "We didn't come to buy bait. Is your brother Sonny home?"

"Oh yes, ma'am!" He clapped his big hands and yanked her door open. "Sonny came this afternoon with a girl. Don't think she's his girlfriend, though." He took hold of Amanda's arm and literally dragged her from the car.

When Sara tried to intervene, he called, "You come, too, ma'am. We don't get much company, so you're more than welcome."

As Will hauled Amanda into the cedar forest, she looked over her shoulder and watched Sara hustling to keep up, her sandals catching in the weeds of an overgrown driveway. The weeds had been recently bent by the passage of a vehicle. When they finally entered a clearing, Amanda saw the blue van, a rusty single-wide trailer, and Pamlico Sound just beyond, with high waves pounding the beach.

Off to the left was Will's digging pit, a ten-foot square of upturned earth fertilized with coffee grounds, eggshells, and all manner of garbage attractive to worms. He had left his shovel plunged in the soil and a plastic resin chair sat beside a plank on concrete blocks. Rows of white cardboard takeout boxes were carefully lined up on the plank, waiting to receive their wiggling product.

Sara caught up, and Amanda longed to take her hand as they approached the trailer's steel door.

Will rapped sharply before entering. "Hey, bro, we got company!" He held the door open so the women could enter first.

When Amanda stepped into the dim room, Sara right behind her, she was aware of several floor fans blowing competing breezes that smelled of beef stew. The space was surprisingly neat, with an uncluttered dining room table, sofa against the far wall, and an expertly fanned-out display of sports magazines on the coffee table. She saw movement on the screen of a big-screen TV in one corner, but other than that, the place seemed deserted.

"Don't be shy now, c'mon in," Will urged.

Only then did she notice the frail figure emerging from a galley kitchen. Tammy Tillman was a shrunken version of her former self. She had on the same outfit she'd worn that day at the lighthouse and her dishwater-blond hair hadn't been washed in days. As she nervously twisted her hands together, her terrified blue eyes were fixed on a spot behind their backs.

"Are you okay, Tammy?" Sara called to her.

When she didn't respond, Amanda tried to draw her out. "We met your father and Elyse today. The kids were helping Leo refinish a boat."

She sensed movement behind her. Sara spun around, her mouth open in a silent scream as Sonny Roach stepped out from behind the opened door. His bloodshot eyes glittered with malice as he aimed his gun at them.

# CHAPTER FORTY-TWO

*Dominoes...*

Amanda and Sara scrambled backward away from Sonny, as though putting distance between them could actually stop a bullet.

"Sonny, no!" Tammy screamed. "What are you doing?"

Even Will seemed shocked as he raised his hands high. "Where'd you get that gun? Can I see it?"

Amanda couldn't speak at all. She'd been here before. The old wound in her side began to throb, and the painful memory was so visceral that only terror kept her from fainting. Sara must have sensed it, because she looped her arm around Amanda, lending support.

"You two just keep on turnin' up." Sonny sighed in exasperation. "Why can't you leave us alone?"

"What do they want, Sonny?" Will asked, yet he was more fascinated by the weapon than alarmed by the situation. Like a little boy, he reached out to touch its shiny cylinder, but his brother slapped his hand away.

"It's time for you to leave, Willy." Sonny gave him a rough shove toward the door. "You best get your damn Chinese food boxes into the boathouse, or else they'll melt in the rain."

The thought so panicked Will that he almost tripped in his rush outside. The high wind nearly tore the screen from its hinges at his exit.

"Stay put in the boathouse 'til I say, you hear?" Sonny screamed at Will's retreating back, but his eyes never left the women. "He won't be back," he chuckled.

Sara spoke up. "My friend is sick. Can we sit down?" Her voice shook so badly, her teeth chattered.

Pointing with the barrel of his gun, Sonny waved them toward the couch. "Make yourselves at home. No one's goin' anywhere anytime soon."

"You don't need to do this, Sonny. Please let them go!" Tammy whimpered, still cowering near the kitchen.

"Hey, darlin', why don't you bake us a cake or something? That's your thing, right?"

But Tammy was frozen to the spot, her eyes darting uncontrollably from person to person. Amanda let Sara lower her to the fake leather couch. When Sara slumped down beside her, she felt her shivering where their skin touched. Surely this was all a bad dream, or a nightmare case of déjà vu. She even recognized Sonny's gun, a Raven MP-25 pistol—like the one she owned. She had fired it only once, the day she got shot, and nearly killed her attacker. After that, she'd put it away for good.

Tammy tried again. "Use your head, Sonny. They don't know anything, so let them leave now, no harm done."

His harsh laughter sent Tammy cringing deeper into the kitchen. "These women know way more than they should." He pointed his gun at Amanda. "This one here? She's like a bitch with a bone. She just won't let go."

"Did you hit me?" Suddenly Amanda found her voice. "Were you down on the beach that night?" She feared she could answer her own question as she realized it was that same night when someone planted Lynette's body in the shipwreck.

But Sonny said, "Hit you? What the hell are you talking about?"

Sara quietly shook her head and urgently squeezed Amanda's hand. Clearly she wanted her to shut up. Likely that was a good idea.

"Don't talk to her, Sonny. It'll make it worse," Tammy spoke from the shadows.

"You afraid your girlfriends here will find out you're in it up to your eyeballs?" He snorted in disgust. "Why don't you make yourself useful and bring me another beer?"

Amanda glanced at Sara as they shared the same question: what was Tammy into up to her eyeballs? Suddenly it seemed possible that they had no allies here. Had Sara been right all along? Was Tammy one of the bad guys? The thought was so devastating that Amanda refused to believe it. But the only thing that mattered now was the loaded gun. When Tammy brought the beer, refusing to look at them, Amanda saw several empties already on the floor beside the sagging armchair, where Sonny then took a seat. How long had the man been drinking? Alcohol and a lethal weapon—not a good combination.

He sat with the Raven in one hand, the bottle in the other, and stared at them. His knees were splayed open, giving them a good look at his crotch. If this was his best shot at intimidation, it was working. Amanda was petrified. Why hadn't he shot them yet, if that was his plan?

"What do you want, Sonny?" Sara quietly asked, surprising Amanda.

About then, buckets of rocks hit the trailer's tin roof.

"Damn hail!" Sonny roared as the house shook and rattled like a jar of marbles. When the barrage stopped, an eerie stillness descended and the smell of ozone filled the room.

"What do you want, Sonny?" Sara gently repeated.

What did Sara hope to accomplish? Only moments before, she had urged Amanda to shut up. But Sara was the shrink. Maybe she knew what she was doing.

The quiet deepened until Sonny hollered for another beer. Once provided, and after Tammy again scampered into hiding like a terrified mouse, the silence became a living, breathing weight pressing down on Amanda's chest. Was that how therapists did it?

Sure enough, when she was ready to scream, Sonny lifted his face, and shockingly, his eyes were filled with tears as he fixed on Sara.

"I want everyone to know it was an accident. I didn't mean to kill her."

The stark words scattered like beads cut off their strand, and each carried the ring of truth.

Again Sara waited several beats too long. "How did it happen, Sonny?"

He put his gun down on the side table and roughly wiped his eyes with the back of his hand. "Lynette was pissed. I've never seen her so mad." This time when he lifted his head, the tears were gone but his mouth was contorted with rage. "If you two hadn't gone to the sheriff with your fuckin' bullshit, Lynette would never have found out."

She was relieved that Sonny was poking an angry finger at them, instead of his gun. Sara was clearly encouraging his rant, not only to elicit information, but also to burn out the fire consuming him.

"How did Lynette find out?" Sara prompted.

"Are you kidding me?" he hollered. "You took your accusations to fuckin' Doyle, and then he went over to screw with Lynette. He came to our house Monday before I got home for lunch, and by the time he left, Lynette was ready to kill herself—or me!"

Amanda listened carefully, trying to piece it together. It seemed Doyle had confronted Lynette about something, maybe their accusations of identity theft? In any case, Lynette had been furious. Sonny also implied that Tammy was somehow involved. The kids were away at day camp, and things got out of hand.

As Sonny continued to bare his soul, the escalating wind rattled the windows of their precarious shelter.

"So we argued, and I pushed her," Sonny confessed. "She hit her head on the edge of the counter and she was gone—nothing I could do to save her."

It seemed the man wanted their absolution. As his words became more slurred, it was plain he was working himself up to a crisis. All they could do was watch in terrified fascination as he began lining his empty bottles up on the floor like a row of upended dominoes. Amanda yearned to ask him why he left Lynette's body lying on the kitchen floor for hours before moving it to the beach. How could he leave the woman he professed to love abandoned and exposed in the watery grave where Amanda found her? But God help her if she dared to ask those questions.

As the seconds stretched like hours, her heart raced as she pictured their deaths. Sonny had told them too much, so they would have to die. He would bury them in Will's worm pit, beneath the garbage and coffee grounds. The image was revolting. So in spite of the fear buzzing in her head, she began calculating the distance between herself and the gun.

She knew how to fire the damn thing. She'd done it before. But her knees were rubber and her hands shook so badly she couldn't be sure she could pull the trigger. Yet Sonny had entered a maniacal, trance-like state as he played with his bottles. And Sara's precious life was at stake. She felt Sara's warmth and sensed her heartbeat, while salvation was only four steps across the room.

As she prepared to lunge, three things happened at once. Tammy ran toward them screaming as the trailer door blew open. Amanda sprang to her feet and was almost to the gun, when the room exploded with sound and light. Finally, Sonny fell forward from his chair, his weight toppling Amanda.

Blood pumped from a perfect blooming rose in the center of his forehead and soaked her lap. His shocked, dead eyes accused her from the pulpy mush that had been his face, just before she blacked out.

# CHAPTER FORTY-THREE

*An officer of the law…*

The persistent scream pushed through Amanda's subconscious until it finally awakened her from an undulating red-and-black chaos. She identified the screamer—Tammy—and felt hands cupping her head—Sara.

"God, Mandy, were you hit?"

She felt Sara's tears on her cheek, and when she opened her eyes, she saw the blurry outline of Sara's dark hair framing her pale face. She rolled free of the heavy weight pinning her lower body.

"The bullet was a through-and-through. It lodged in the coffee table. Never hit her," a strange male voice said.

Slowly she moved her legs and flexed her fingers. Everything seemed to work, but she was disoriented, like coming out of anesthesia. When her lips moved, sound came out. "What happened?"

"You've only been out a few minutes." Sara continued to stroke and examine her body, convincing herself that Amanda was indeed unharmed. When the screaming stopped, Sara said, "Tammy, bring me a warm, wet washcloth and a towel."

Soon Sara was bathing her face, arms, hands, legs, and rubbing her with the towel. It was then the horror returned. "Did I kill Sonny?" she sobbed.

"No, babe."

"I shot him, Miss Rittenhouse. It seems I got here just in the nick of time."

This time the voice was familiar. Leveraging on her elbows, she blinked and squinted at the man in a brown uniform. It was comforting to have an officer of the law present, until she focused and saw his red hair.

"It's Deputy Doyle," Sara urgently whispered in her ear. "He's here to help us."

Even incapacitated, Amanda knew the part about Doyle helping them was wishful thinking. Perhaps by speaking it aloud, Sara hoped to appeal to his better angels.

"Don't count on Doyle," she warned under her breath.

Along with the towel and washcloth, Tammy had brought a sheet. Without ceremony, she spread it over the gory corpse of Sonny Roach. By the sneer of disgust and loathing on Tammy's face, the scream she'd uttered at Sonny's demise was shock, not sorrow. In fact, by the time Tammy had washed her hands at the kitchen sink, she had transformed from a mouse to a mountain lion, and her smug smile betrayed not one ounce of sympathy for her mother's murdered boyfriend.

Amanda considered Sonny's death a murder. Yes, Sonny had harbored vile intentions, and she herself had been going for his gun, but coming in from the outside, Doyle could not have known these things. Yet he shot Sonny in cold blood, in the back of his head, while to all appearances, the man was sitting peacefully in his armchair. The fact made her skin crawl.

"He would have killed you," Doyle said suddenly in his own defense, as though he had read her mind.

"We owe you our lives," Sara solemnly agreed.

Why was Sara pandering to this killer? Amanda figured there was a method to her madness, but her obsequiousness was sickening. As she allowed Sara to help her to her feet, it also occurred to her that when she'd seen him snoring in his truck on the ferry, he'd been wearing a touristy-looking Hawaiian shirt, but now he was in uniform with his badge, cuffs, and gun. But why? He'd had been suspended from duty, but folks on Ocracoke didn't know that. Perhaps he figured the uniform's authority would elevate him above reproach so no one would question his actions—no matter how outrageous they might be.

"You're a mess, Mandy." Tammy shook her head.

It was true. Though Sara had done a credible job cleaning her skin, her shirt and shorts were soaked with Sonny's blood. The idea made her feel faint all over again. She desperately needed a shower, but she figured a change of clothes was the best she could hope for. "Do you have anything I can wear?"

"My suitcase is at Daddy's house, but I'll try to find something in Will's closet," she grudgingly offered. Moments later, she returned with a pair of men's khaki shorts and an oversize white T-shirt. "I suppose you can change in the bedroom."

"Wait!" Doyle called. "Take Sonny's gun and go with her, Tammy. We don't want Miss Rittenhouse disappearing out the back door." He handed her the Raven MP-25.

Not a good sign.

"That's not necessary," Sara objected.

He shrugged. "Can't be too careful, ma'am. It's for her protection."

"Sorry, Mandy," Tammy mumbled, tucking the pistol into her waistband as they moved down a short hall to the bedroom. Like the living room, it was also neat—tightly made bed, shoes lined up on the floor, no litter of dirty clothes.

It made her wonder about Will. "Is Sonny's brother still in the boathouse? You would think the gunshot would have brought him running."

"Will's a little slow," Tammy answered dismissively.

Most lesbians would modestly look away while an acquaintance changed her clothes, but Tammy wasn't a lesbian, so Amanda had no opportunity to go for the gun.

As they returned to the living room, she couldn't decide which was worse—bloody clothes, or shorts that threatened to fall off her hips at the slightest provocation and a T-shirt that accentuated the details of her braless breasts. She'd asked Tammy to burn everything if she got a chance, including her bra, deciding that even ill-fitting clothes were better than the depressing alternative. But when Doyle stared pointedly at her chest, she wasn't so sure.

Under different circumstances, Sara would have laughed at her attire, but at the moment she was again seated on the fake leather couch and found no humor in their predicament.

"Now that we're all together again," Doyle began, "I'll be needing your cell phones." He held out his hand.

Sara obligingly lifted hers from the pocket of her shorts and handed it over. Amanda opened her purse and relinquished only her phone, while hoping against hope that Tammy's phone would remain concealed in her bag's zippered pocket.

"Mandy is hiding something. Give me your bag," Tammy demanded. She may not have been a lesbian, but every woman knows her way around a purse. In less than a minute, she found her phone. "Jesus, this is mine! Where did you find it?" Her blue eyes expanded in surprise and delight.

"It was under your pillow in Mooresville." Amanda figured she had nothing to lose.

"Shit! You searched my house? Did you see how Sonny trashed the place?"

Maybe she had something to lose after all. Amanda decided to keep her big mouth shut.

"I suppose you guessed that Sonny was after the drug money? You heard him ask me for the cash at Ginny's wedding." Tammy seemed furious. "Did you tell the cops about that, too?"

"I don't know what you're talking about." Except that Tammy had just admitted that the cash was drug money.

"She's lying, Rusty. Mandy needs to practice her poker face."

Fortunately, Sara came to the rescue. She put on her neutral therapist face. "Calm down, Tammy. I promise you, Mandy didn't tell the cops anything, because we don't know anything. We all need to sit down and talk about this. You should tell Deputy Doyle how Sonny confessed to killing your mother, and—"

"He did?" Doyle interrupted. "Roach admitted he murdered your old mama? Son of a bitch!" He kicked Sonny's shroud with the toe of his polished boot. "The sheriff's gonna give me a medal."

"Don't do that, Rusty," Tammy said half-heartedly.

"No really, think about it. We've solved a homicide here. I told Lynette the truth, doll. About you and Roach? She must have freaked when she got her hands on him."

"Shut up, Rusty!"

Clearly Tammy had transferred her rage from Amanda to Doyle.

He winked at Tammy and squared his shoulders. Obviously he was extremely proud of himself. He crossed the narrow room to a small picture window beside the couch and tentatively opened the Venetian blinds. "Shit, what a mess!"

Since she was still standing, Amanda was able to peer over Sara's shoulder and see leaves plastered against the window. Although it was fully dark outside, the glow from the interior revealed that a large tree had fallen behind the trailer. A few feet closer and it would have smashed them. At the same time, the violent storm had abated.

"It's only a lull," he added. "In another hour or so, it'll spiral around and hit us again."

"Maybe we should leave now while we still have the chance?" Sara suggested.

For several seconds, he seemed to consider the proposal, but as Amanda watched his face, she was terrified by what she saw. At first he looked confused, possibly even frightened. His lips moved in a face so pale each freckle stood out like dots on a chalkboard. He was talking to himself, reasoning it out in his head. Then his eyes began to shift and focus with resolve as his complexion turned red.

"Not a good idea," he muttered.

"What should we do, Rusty?" Even Tammy was alarmed by his strange transformation.

"We need to clean up this mess!" he shouted.

He was unhinged. As Amanda's legs threatened to buckle, she moved to sit beside Sara, thinking that by settling herself in the charged atmosphere, the situation would de-escalate. But before she reached the couch, he grabbed her arm.

"No, no, no!" he yelled. "Don't get comfortable. You're going out!" His fingers bit into her skin, and when she dared to look into his eyes, he took hold of her shoulders and viciously shook her. "No, no, no! Don't argue with me!"

She hadn't said a word. Was he crazy? By then Sara was on her feet, clawing at his arms, begging him to release Amanda. She managed to get his right hand loose, but then he slapped her across the face. Amanda moaned when she saw the red imprint of his fingers on Sara's cheeks and tears spilling from her eyes.

"Stop it!" she screamed as she punched him.

Tammy intervened. "Leave them alone, Rusty!"

Only Tammy's words stopped his attack. His arms dropped and hung limp at his sides. His eyes glazed over and an inappropriate smile curved his lips. "Sorry," he panted. "But you girls have to leave now. Help me, Tammy."

"What the hell are we doing?" Tammy's eyes were enormous, but she obediently followed as he shoved first Sara, then Amanda, toward the front door.

"Take out the gun, Tammy, and follow behind us. If either woman tries to run, shoot her."

# CHAPTER FORTY-FOUR

*The boathouse...*

He pushed them out into the night. The ground was mushy and awash with puddles. It soaked and sucked at Amanda's sandals as they stumbled through debris. When Doyle produced a tiny flashlight, its bright halogen beam exposed the devastation—fallen branches, upended lawn furniture, scattered buckets, and tangled clotheslines.

"Jesus Christ!" Tammy tripped along behind them. "Where are we going?"

The beam pinpointed a metal building down near the shore. "Boathouse," he muttered.

"But Willy's in the boathouse," Tammy objected.

"I don't think so." Doyle giggled as he continued to shove them onward toward the structure.

"But where would he go?" Tammy asked. "Willy can't drive."

"Maybe he took off on his bicycle?" He picked up the pace.

One of Amanda's shoes pulled off in the muck and she nearly fell. When she reached down to retrieve it, he jerked her upright.

"Leave it!" he shouted.

Sara took her hand and helped steady her. "Do as he says, and we'll be all right," she whispered and didn't let go of her hand.

She nodded miserably, although she was sure Sara couldn't see her. Since it was impossible to walk in only one sandal, she toed the other off and left it behind. She prayed she wouldn't step on a snake, rusty nail, or something even more lethal. Clearly he was insane, because she could think of no good reason for this trek to the boathouse. Was it too much to hope that Will Roach would be lurking there to save them, to avenge the death of his brother? More likely he'd been beaten with his own shovel, and he was the one lying in the worm pit. The idea made her dizzy, like she'd had the wind knocked out of her.

By the time Doyle opened the back door of the boathouse, the wind and rain had picked up, while the ocean roared not far beyond the steel enclosure. He flicked a switch, which flooded the space with cold fluorescent light.

The room was about twelve feet wide and twenty-five feet deep, a framework with an electric garage door at the ocean end. The concrete slab floor had been poured to include two sets of wide tracks to guide a boat trailer. The trailer itself, attached to a winch, was empty. And so was the building. No Will to save them. And if Sonny's brother had departed by sea in the missing boat, then he was surely in Davey Jones' Locker.

Doyle shoved them inside and Tammy followed with the gun dangling at the end of her right arm. "Now what?" she sighed as she brushed the soaked, dishwater-blond hair from her eyes.

He seemed unsure about the next move. As he stood, blinking with indecision, Amanda calmed herself by looking around. Like everything else, Will's boathouse was well organized, with fishing rods, oars, fenders, life jackets and other marine gear neatly racked on the walls. Three small floor fans valiantly rotated in a futile attempt to cool the humid space, which stank of seaweed and dead fish. He had a space heater, a small cooking stove, and a sturdy metal-frame single bed made up against a side wall. She supposed this had once been his retreat, when the Roach clan was still alive and kicking.

"C'mon, Rusty, do something," Tammy whined. "Shouldn't we call 911 and tell them about Sonny?"

He took a perfectly ironed handkerchief from a pocket and mopped his pink face. "Let me think…"

"You know the cops will understand. You had to shoot him," Tammy said.

Only then did he snap from his fugue state. "Shut up, Tammy! They'll never understand!" At the same moment, a deafening clap of thunder shook the walls. "Besides, don't you think the cops have better things to do during a hurricane emergency?"

*Better than responding to a brutal murder?* Amanda wondered bitterly. But then he grabbed her arm in one hand, Sara's in the other, and walked them stumbling toward the narrow metal bed.

"Sit down, damn it!"

Before they could comply, he shoved them both onto the mattress.

"What are you doing?" Sara shrieked as he pulled off her shoes and tossed them across the room.

He removed a set of steel handcuffs from his belt. "Lie down, feet up on the bed!"

Sara tried to fight, but he slapped her face again. When Amanda balled her fist and gave her best shot to his jaw, he howled in rage, and then punched her in the belly. The blow landed precisely in her gut where she'd been wounded, and it hurt like hell.

"Help me here, Tammy!" he shouted as he wrestled them down onto the bed. "Get them side-by-side on their backs."

Tammy could have rebelled at that moment, but she cried instead. She held down Amanda's shoulders and batted Sara's flailing hands as he snapped a cuff around Amanda's right ankle and shoved her against the wall. He then threaded the second cuff through an upright bar in the footboard, and locked the other cuff around Sara's left ankle, rendering them helpless as turtles on their backs.

"You won't get away with this!" Sara sobbed.

He calmly stood up and fussed with the crease in his trousers leg. Tammy was still crying as they backed away from the bed. "Tammy, you have to help us!" she pleaded.

But she just continued weeping and stared down at her shoes. Soon their captors moved toward the door. "Can we at least leave the lights on for them?" she asked in a meek voice.

He laughed. "Sure, I'm a reasonable man." And then he looked at them and said, "Shut up, you two. You dykes like sleeping together, right? So what's the problem?"

He slammed the door and locked it.

# CHAPTER FORTY-FIVE

*Worst-case scenario...*

When they were gone, neither she nor Sara was capable of speech. Instead they cried and held hands, trying to find a workable position with their ankles so closely shackled. In the end, they could only lie flat on their backs, with Amanda's right leg pressed against the length of Sara's left. They had to work their bare feet through the vertical bars in the footboard to take the painful pressure off the stretched cuffs. The exhaustive effort would have been comical, had it not been so desperate. And when they finally got somewhat comfortable, she didn't know whether to laugh or cry.

"So this is what it means to be joined at the hip?" she said through her tears. Sara strangled out a laugh, but Amanda knew the joke wasn't funny. She twisted around on her right hip so she could loop her arm around Sara. "If I hold you really tight, can you scooch over and snag the pillow from the floor?"

"What?" Sara's bloodshot eyes darted back and forth until she finally understood her request. "You want the pillow?"

"Yes, can you reach it?"

Carefully shifting onto her right hip, as Amanda had done, Sara was able to use her left arm to get the pillow. She dragged it onto the bed, shoved it under their heads, and almost fell off in the process. "Better..." she gasped. "I adore you, babe, but this is a little too close for comfort."

By the manic giggle in Sara's voice, Amanda realized she had lost her legendary cool. She wanted to ask her if she was okay, but the question was preposterous. If she felt anything like Amanda, all she wanted to do was curl up and cry until the world disappeared.

She closed her eyes and listened to the wind screaming through the tortured cedar forest and lashing the roof. Beyond the garage door, the raging ocean crept closer. When she craned her neck, she saw a stream of water leaking into the building.

"We've gotta get out of here, Sara."

"Let me think..."

She held Sara tighter, felt her heart beating under her hand, and tasted the salty sweetness when she kissed the back of her neck. "What is he waiting for?" she moaned. "If he intends to kill us, why doesn't he just do it?"

Speaking her worst fear aloud somehow made it real. In spite of the oppressive heat, she began to shiver. In response, Sara wriggled onto her back and searched her eyes.

"No one else is going to die, Mandy. I won't let that happen." Sara stroked her back. "Doyle is out of control, but he's not crazy. Maybe he can justify killing Sonny, but he could never explain hurting us."

She desperately wanted to believe, but unlike Sara, she thought Doyle was crazy. And unfortunately she had already constructed a worst-case scenario. "I think he plans to shoot us with Sonny's gun and then tell everyone Sonny did it. He'll claim he had to kill Sonny to end his rampage."

As soon as the words left her mouth, she bitterly regretted it. Sara stopped stroking her back and stared, a look of pure panic on her face. The theory was plausible, brilliant even. A psychopath like Doyle could pull it off and come out a hero.

"How can that work, with Sonny dead up at the trailer and us out here in the boathouse?" Sara vigorously shook her head.

The real question was how could they lie there, like sacrificial lambs chained to their slab, and speculate about their own murders?

"Besides," Sara continued hopefully, "Tammy would never let him harm us. I know her. She may have been involved with the drug deals and identity scams, but she would never condone murder."

Again, Amanda kept her mouth shut, not wanting to point out that even as her shrink, Sara had failed to learn the truth about Tammy. And if love was a factor, if Tammy still hoped to marry Doyle, then she'd stand by her man no matter what. Amanda tenderly traced the contours of Sara's face. Her cheeks were still wet with tears.

"Maybe you're right, but I think we need a Plan B."

# CHAPTER FORTY-SIX

*Contortionists...*

Sara sighed deeply as her eyes roved restlessly around the boathouse. "If we had a bobby pin, a paperclip, or a thin shim of metal like a credit card, then I could bust us out of these damn handcuffs."

"My God, are you for real? Where did you learn such a skill?" Suddenly she forgot to be scared shitless.

Sara laughed. "I hang with a rough crowd, remember? Some of my ex-felons have clued me in to all kinds of trade secrets while they spill their guts on my couch. For some reason, this one stuck."

"It stuck because you thought you might need to escape from handcuffs if you ever met a woman into S&M?"

This time Sara laughed even harder and tweaked Amanda's nose. The horrible tension was broken, so they both got busy scanning the premises for possible lockpicks. At the same moment, a heavy limb crashed onto the roof directly above the bed, and they nearly jumped out of their skins. Amanda anxiously examined the ceiling, looking for a fatal breach. The metal was punched in like a sagging hammock, but the roof still held. Then she spotted a rack of fishing rods up near the ceiling.

"Sara, would a fishhook work?"

"Maybe, but how the hell can we get to the rods?"

"Give me the pillow!" She and her brother Robby had been infamous childhood pillow fighters, but she was the champ. "I'll have one down in no time."

She had bragged too soon, for it took eight attempts before two rods rained down. Luckily they landed within reach and Sara was able to get both. The first offered only bobbers, but the second had a large substantial hook stretched back at the end of the line and anchored into the rod's cork handle.

"It might work." Sara dug at the knot and soon had the evil-looking hook free. "Wish I had some wire cutters. I don't want these barbs, only the straight shaft."

"Give it to me." She threaded the shaft through a small hole in the reel so the barbs jammed in the spool of line. Then she was able to twist and bend it until the shaft finally broke off. "How's this?" she crowed.

"You are a woman of many talents. Now, if only I were double-jointed, this would be a lot easier. Move over while I scoot forward."

She flattened her body against the wall, while Sara sat up, her right foot braced on the floor, her left knee folded up under her chin so she could twist her shackled ankle inward with its tiny round keyhole upright.

"Ouch!" Her ankle pulled against the hard steel. "We should be contortionists."

"Hang on. I'll do this as fast as I can." Sara manipulated the shaft around inside the keyhole. "Now, I think we're almost there. When I wiggle this into the hole next time, I should be able to lift the locking device and click the cuffs open."

"Please hurry!" The restraint was cutting into Amanda's skin. At the same time, the wind began grinding their little shelter like a demonic can opener. Glass shattered as two windows blew inward from the far wall. Seconds later, the garage door shrieked as it was torn off its hinges and carried away into the night. Finally, an explosion thundered through the cedar forest, leaving them in total darkness.

Their screams ricocheted through what was left of the boathouse, which miraculously, still retained its roof. And for an eternity, the violence of windblown objects flew through the bones of their space as they covered their heads with their arms. Then, just as suddenly, the wind died.

"Are you okay, Sara?" Her voice was a hoarse whisper.

Sara moaned. "I dropped the damn lock pick! Now the floor is covered with water and I'll never find it."

She was just grateful they were still alive. It now seemed the hurricane was a greater threat than Deputy Doyle. She gently stroked Sara's tense legs, urging them out of their twisted position to lie flat on the mattress, easing the strain on their cuffed ankles. In the muggy stillness that followed, all she heard was the muffled sound of Sara trying to choke back tears. Even the electric floor fans had ceased their slow rotation, making the silence even more absolute.

"I wish the lights would come back on," Amanda said.

"No, you don't, babe." Sara shakily found her hand. "Those fans are sitting in the same water as our metal bed. The water conducts electricity, so the darkness is our friend."

# CHAPTER FORTY-SEVEN

*Into the abyss…*

They sank deeper and deeper into a place where all tears were cried out and exhaustion was so profound that only one escape was possible. They fell asleep. Amanda went gratefully into the abyss, and when morning came, she fought the consciousness that dragged her into an improbable new world of sunshine and surviving songbirds.

The sensation was like surfacing from under water, but instead of sweet oxygen, her lungs expanded with a breath of horror. They were clinging too tightly to one another, bathed in each other's sweat.

Sara startled awake soon after, gasping with the same horror. "Oh God!" she intoned. But her words were less like a prayer, more like a curse.

"Well, at least the power didn't come on." Amanda could think of nothing more hopeful to say as she inched out of Sara's sweet, suffocating embrace.

"At least we didn't wash out to sea." Sara pushed the moist mane of dark hair off her face and reared up on one elbow. She looked around in disbelief at the destruction of the boathouse. Approximately six inches of salt water, seaweed, and several dead fish sloshed around the legs of their bed. "At least if we get hungry, we have fresh sushi."

She groaned. Perhaps they had died and gone to absurdist heaven, and none of this was real. "Or we could each gnaw off our bound foot, lose the cuffs and hop out of here."

At that, Sara flopped back down onto their pillow and gently took Amanda's face into her hands. "We will get out of here, with all four feet—I promise."

The lie sounded so good from Sara's lips that Amanda sealed it with a kiss. A sensation of peace followed, or perhaps it was resignation. "Maybe Tammy and Doyle left, and the good guys will get here soon."

"Sure, or maybe Aqua will swoop down in her helicopter, just like she said, and rescue us."

Wouldn't it be pretty to think so? She thought about the big bed waiting for them at Blackbeard's Lodge, about the four-poster back at Jo's—all the places they could have been instead, had it not been for her pigheaded obsession with Tammy.

"I'm so sorry, Sara." She touched her cheek.

"It's not your fault, so don't even go there. We both got us into this mess, and we'll get out together."

As they gazed into one another's eyes, Amanda willing Sara's words to be true, the back door to the boathouse creaked open and Doyle walked in, Tammy right behind him. "I guess they didn't leave after all."

"Wow, looks like a hurricane tore through here!" He smiled as he approached them in high rubber boots. Tammy was wearing them too. "It's even worse outside," he continued. "Like World War Three."

"Tammy, when are we getting out?" Sara ignored him completely. "We won't press charges if you release us now, but if you don't, I will personally make sure they throw the book at you."

Amanda couldn't see how they were in any position to bargain, but she noticed that Tammy looked away in shame.

She also noticed Sonny's gun was still tucked into the waistband of Tammy's jeans, so she again prepared for the worst-case scenario.

"Hope you slept well, ladies," he continued conversationally. "Tammy and I didn't get a wink."

What was wrong with the man? Had he fallen all the way off his rocker? And who cared how they spent the night? She assumed they'd used the time to dispose of Sonny's body, or mop up blood, or stage the perfect crime scene for a new double homicide—theirs. She watched carefully as he removed a tiny key from his breast pocket and leaned over the bed.

"Are you two getting tired of the Siamese twin routine?" He laughed. "Hope you can still walk, because we need to get you back to the house."

Instead of rejoicing at his intention to remove the cuffs, Sara was still fixated on Tammy. "Why are you wearing rubber gloves?"

She didn't answer Sara's question, but she wore the blue latex throwaway gloves nurses used. Either she really had been mopping blood, or she didn't want to leave fingerprints or get powder blowback when she fired Sonny's Raven. As her neck and cheeks turned red, she stared into the fouled water swirling around her boots, as though the belly-up fish floating there were the most fascinating sight she'd ever seen.

Doyle answered for her as he roughly grabbed Sara's left ankle, getting the angle right to insert the key. "Tammy's wearing boots as well as gloves. It's nasty out there, ladies. The island runs on wells and septic tanks, and much of it is below sea level. When it floods, you don't want to walk around in sewage, do you?"

Vivid and disgusting as that was, it still didn't explain Tammy's gloves. As he removed her cuffs, Amanda flexed her raw ankle and wondered about logistics. Had they wiped Sonny's gun clean, pressed it into his cold, dead hand, and arranged his limp finger on the trigger for fresh prints? Then had Tammy put on gloves to keep from contaminating the evidence that would nail Sonny for their murders?

Her heart raced as she imagined their deaths. She couldn't catch her breath, nor could she stand on her numb right leg when he shoved her lower body over the edge of the bed. Only when the vile water washed over her bare feet did she notice that Sara was resisting. She was fighting like a wildcat. When he tried to make her stand, she scratched at his eyes and clawed at his arms. "We're not going anywhere, asshole!" she screamed.

So Amanda decided it was in her best interest to resist too. Since her left leg still worked, she cocked her knee and kicked him in the crotch. The effect was loud and immediate, as he doubled over, squealing and cupping his balls.

"Help us, Tammy!" Sara cried. "You know he's going to kill us!"

He was disabled but he wasn't out of the game. Complicating matters, neither she nor Sara had the ability to walk, let alone run. Fighting back had landed them both back on the bed, helpless.

"Please, Tammy!" Sara pleaded as they struggled upright. "Think about your brother and sister. What will Roger and Susan do if you go to prison?"

Tammy mumbled something about the kids living with their grandpa Leo, but her words were hard to understand. She turned toward Doyle. "We don't have to do this, Rusty," she sobbed. "If we stop now, we'll be okay."

"Have you lost your mind, Tammy? They'll crucify me on the drugs and you on the identity thefts, and these bitches are the ones who will nail us to the cross." He drew his service revolver and pointed it at Amanda's chest. He was still bent like a pretzel, coughing and choking so hard she feared the gun would go off accidentally.

If Amanda's theory was correct, though, he wouldn't use his gun. He'd wait to do the deed with Sonny's. Better yet, he'd have Tammy shoot them. On the other hand, she had no reason to believe her scenario had any basis in reality. While these thoughts raced through her brain at lightning speed, she'd failed to notice that Sara had lowered herself into a semi-crouch, her butt braced against the bed's headboard.

When she sprang into action, Sara's karate chop to Doyle's neck, coupled with a spin kick to his battered groin, stunningly crippled the man. He dropped his weapon and shrieked as he hit the floor.

"Shoot them now, Tammy!" he screamed before his face went under water.

In the chaos, Amanda reached for his gun. As she bent over, adrenaline pumping overtime, she saw Sara holding his face under water with her good foot, while he clasped Sara's bad ankle with his strong right hand. He tugged with all his might, and Sara toppled backward onto Amanda, preventing her from claiming his gun.

He came up, sputtering and furious. "What are you waiting for, Tammy? Pull the damn trigger!"

While Amanda and Sara struggled for their footing on the slimy floor, he crabbed on all fours and retrieved his weapon. In the movies, guns still fired after submersion in water, but was that true in real life? Amanda didn't want to find out, because when she looked up, the muzzle of his gun was pointed at her face, and Tammy had finally heeded his orders. She had assumed a wide-legged stance, with Sonny's Raven steadied in both hands, arms locked and extended. From Amanda's vantage point, Tammy was aiming at the back of Sara's head.

In that suspended moment, as she prepared to die, Amanda locked eyes with Sara, hoping to convey the enormity of her love and sorrow.

And then the shot rang out.

# CHAPTER FORTY-EIGHT

*The key…*

*The profound silence of the grave.* The phrase repeated like a prayerful mantra as Amanda listened to gently moving water, labored breathing, and most audible—a pathetic whimpering as she slowly opened her eyes. Even before her lids lifted, she knew she hadn't passed out. She wasn't dead or even hurt, and only a few seconds had elapsed since the gunshot.

"Are you hurt, Sara?" When she crawled around, Sara was on her knees, holding Doyle.

"Did I kill him?" Tammy moaned, with Sonny's gun hanging at the end of her limp arm.

"Get over here and help us!" Sara commanded. "I need you, too, Mandy."

As reality sharpened into focus, she realized Tammy had saved their lives. She went into action, helping Sara and Tammy hoist Doyle out of the water and onto the bed. He was very much alive, moaning and groping his backside as they rolled him onto his belly.

"Jesus, Tammy," Amanda giggled hysterically. "You shot him in the butt!"

Tammy found no humor in the remark as she alternated between weeping and telling Rusty she was sorry. And yet she willingly relinquished her gun to Amanda, removed her rubber gloves, and helped secure her fiancé.

Amanda spotted the hated handcuffs open on the mattress. "Sara, will you do the honors?"

Sara savored her revenge. None too gently, she pulled his right wrist upward and secured it to the headboard. "Bastard!" she muttered.

He watched through eyes glazed with baleful resignation while Tammy fluttered uselessly by his side.

"Tammy, give me your cell phone," Sara demanded. She quickly dug the phone from her pocket and handed it over. "Now please go over to the door and turn the switch off, so that the electricity won't come back on."

Moving like an obedient zombie, Tammy did Sara's bidding. Sara winked at Amanda and handed her Tammy's phone. "It's not like I expect the power to be restored anytime soon, but if it were, we'd all be fried."

Only one bar of charge remained on Tammy's phone, but Amanda dialed 911. She efficiently described the carnage to an incredulous operator, and even managed to supply their address before the phone died. "I think I got their attention," she said.

Having completed her task, Tammy slogged back to them through the water. She held Sara's discarded sandals, one in each hand, like a bedraggled retriever. She gave them to Sara, and looked tearfully at Doyle. "I don't know what happened to Rusty. He was such a sweet boy in high school. He always protected me from..." Her words died in a paroxysm of sobs.

Amanda pitied the woman and tried to fill in the blank. From whom did Tammy need protection—from Sonny, her mother? She flashed on tidbits she knew about Tammy's tumultuous past. Clearly she'd had a difficult home situation when Sonny replaced her father, bringing drugs and addiction into their lives.

Sara had once believed in Tammy, seen something redeemable in the girl. But in the end, Amanda had been the one who'd fought so hard to save Tammy. She felt like the key was just out of reach, the key capable of unlocking the mystery of Tammy's total fall from grace.

"Tammy. I'm curious about something," she gently began. "When your daddy, Leo, moved out and Sonny Roach came to your house, Sonny and your mom became lovers, right?"

Tammy's sobs intensified. "Mama really loved that bastard," she choked.

She sensed Sara's eyes boring into the back of her head, but she continued to press. "Lynette loved Sonny, and he got her pregnant. Then Roger was born, and Sonny was his father."

A look of raw defiance crossed Tammy's face and she abruptly stopped crying. "Yes, Sonny is Roger's daddy," she said haltingly. "But Roger isn't my brother. He's my son."

# CHAPTER FORTY-NINE

*All the way home…*

Amanda rolled away from Sara and stretched luxuriantly between the sheets of their bed at Blackbeard's Lodge. It had been beyond wonderful to enjoy warm showers, shampoo, healing balm for their ankles, and a deep, dreamless sleep after their ordeal. The sheriff's debriefing had taken all of Monday, so that now, Tuesday morning, their only concerns were what to eat, where to eat it, or whether to just spend the day in bed.

"You were amazing, Sara!" Amanda said for the umpteenth time. "Your hands should be registered as lethal weapons." She had seen Sara in action once before, when she'd taken down a drunken coworker intent upon assaulting her. But her karate chop in the boathouse had been a life-and-death save, reminding Amanda that Sara had taken martial arts training many years ago.

"No, *you* were the valiant one," Sara protested. "You kept pushing us to save Tammy, and in the end it paid off, because Tammy saved us."

Yes, Tammy had pulled the trigger and kept them from sure death, but would any of the violence have been necessary if Amanda had left well enough alone? Sara would forever deny she was to blame, but Amanda would always wonder.

"So did Sonny really rape Tammy when she was a teenager?" she asked.

"Of course. Possibly both he and Tammy were high at the time, but he still committed an unforgivable assault on a minor."

She believed the old rape had caused the new violence to cannonball. In Tammy's testimony to her arresting deputy, which she and Sara had witnessed, Tammy confirmed that she, her mom, and recently her sister Susan had used the cover of Mer-Maids to commit identity theft. Tammy broke free of the scam when she moved to Mooresville, but had Lynette lived, she would have eventually groomed Tammy's son Roger to assist in the family business—much like the Artful Dodger trained little Oliver Twist.

Sonny, Doyle, and a foreigner, whom Tammy was too terrified to identify by name, had formed a triumvirate to run the drug trade. The foreigner purchased the product and brought it ashore in his boat. Either Sonny or Doyle, if he was on night patrol, met the foreigner on the beach and received the drugs. As it turned out, Doyle was the one who had attacked Amanda that night when he saw her chasing Tammy. Doyle had been in the middle of a meet with the foreigner when Tammy ran past, oblivious to the deal going down. When Doyle conked Amanda, Tammy just kept on running, but said she remembered hearing some voices.

Sonny was responsible for distributing the product in his tow trucks and collecting money from the customers. Then he gave the cash to Doyle, who parked it with his mom, to eventually be picked up by the foreigner. It was a neat little chain until Tammy broke it by stealing cash she found at the home of Doyle's mama. Tammy claimed to have done this out of spite and hatred of Doyle's mother. She never told Doyle what she had done, but Sonny Roach figured it out. He chased her to Mooresville, then followed her back to the Outer Banks to get it back.

Deputy Doyle's other role had been to keep the sheriff and especially Sergeant Aqua off track, steering their investigation in the wrong direction.

"One could argue," Amanda mused as she trailed her finger along Sara's collarbone, "that Doyle was very effective at keeping Aqua off track. It seems Aqua was right about one thing, though—Doyle did kill Eddie Cutler in self-defense."

"Right. Tammy testified that since she left the Outer Banks, Cutler had become Lynette's right-hand man. He saw Doyle coming with that warrant and panicked, drew his gun, and lost his life."

"Surely Tammy told Doyle all about her family's extracurricular activities," Amanda said. "With that knowledge, he could have arrested both Lynette and Cutler. He had a lot of leverage."

Sara caught her teasing finger and cuddled it under her breasts. "Not exactly. If he loved Tammy at all, and then sank Lynette's boat, then Tammy would have gone down with it."

Amanda ran her hand down Sara's smooth leg and thought about the sad story. Lynette Tillman had always assumed that Rusty Doyle got her sixteen-year-old daughter pregnant. She sent Tammy off to live with Aunt Susan in Mooresville, while she laid low and pretended to be pregnant. Sonny also assumed the illegitimate child was Rusty's. Then when Roger was born, he and Lynette raised the boy as their own, while Tammy stayed on with Aunt Susan.

"I wonder why Tammy didn't tell her mom the truth?" Sara asked as she lazily guided Amanda's hand between her legs.

"Who knows? Maybe she was scared of Sonny? I understand why she didn't want to move home, though, and she was way too young to raise Roger."

According to Doyle's confession, he had blamed Sonny for misplacing the foreigner's cash and decided to confront Lynette. He paid her a visit the morning when Amanda and Sara were picnicking with Aqua on the beach. When Lynette refused to help him, Doyle dealt the most devastating blow possible—he told Lynette how Sonny had raped Tammy, and that Roger was Sonny's son.

At first Lynette had refused to believe his accusation, but when he swore he'd never had sex with Tammy when they were in high school, in an agonized flash of understanding, Lynette saw the truth.

"I can almost visualize the confrontation when Sonny came home," Sara said as she draped her leg over Amanda. "Lynette attacked Sonny. Not only had he betrayed their love by raping her daughter, but he had allowed her to raise Roger, the symbol of Sonny's infidelity. Can you imagine Lynette's guilt? She'd turned a blind eye to her daughter's abuse, then banished Tammy from their home."

"Yes, but look at it from Sonny's point of view. He never knew he had a son. When confronted, it's no wonder he fought back." Amanda slid her fingers farther up Sara's leg. "And if Lynette's death was really an accident, it's even sadder. Because in a perverse way, they both died for love."

"Not a bad way to go," Sara murmured urgently as she guided Amanda all the way home.

# CHAPTER FIFTY

*Epilogue...*

The Friday afternoon of Lynette Tillman's memorial service was fresh and bright, not a cloud in the sky as a small assembly gathered on the beach at Cape Hatteras. The local Baptist church had provided the minister, several dozen white resin chairs facing the sea, and a card table draped with a blue-and-gold cloth to hold the urn with Lynette's ashes.

Amanda and Sara hadn't planned to attend, but since this was their last day on the Outer Banks, and since Aqua was also going to act as Tammy's police escort, the event seemed a perfect exclamation point for the end of their vacation.

They parked their rented Camaro in a lot still awash with salt water and drifted sand. Tropical Storm Bella had never reached hurricane status before coming ashore, or the damage to the islands would have been much worse. But to Amanda and Sara, the devastation had been dramatic enough.

They had caught the first ferry to leave Ocracoke, and as they'd left Blackbeard's Lodge, they had spotted Sonny Roach's brother, Will. He was commiserating with the elderly moocher at the hotel's hospitality station, both men helping themselves to free coffee and doughnuts. They had caught his bloodshot eyes, and he had risen to tell his story—which was quite short. No, he hadn't witnessed his brother's murder. But yes, he had escaped on his bicycle and ridden far away from the trailer before, as he put it, "the shit hit the fan."

Amanda took Sara's arm and they helped one another up and over the damaged dunes to the site of the service. When they reached the crest, she realized with a thump deep in her chest, that the funeral was being held only yards from the shipwreck where she had found Lynette's body. Farther down the beach, the old Frisco Fishing Pier hunkered in dark silhouette against the blinding sun.

"I don't believe it," Amanda whispered as unexpected tears flooded her eyes. Sara understood, no need to explain.

The heels of their new sandals left little impressions in the damp sand as they moved down to the back row of chairs.

"Look, there's Aqua." Sara nodded at their friend, also seated in the back row. Although she was there in an official capacity, she was dressed in civilian clothes, like all the other mourners. Tammy, her prisoner, was seated up front, her head bowed.

"What will happen to Tammy?" Amanda asked as a low-flying flock of seagulls left gray shadows moving across the beach.

Sara sighed. "She will serve a few years in prison, but with good behavior and the mitigating circumstance of her having saved our lives, she'll get out sooner, rather than later."

Amanda gazed out at the waves endlessly licking the shore. At the same time, four more familiar figures passed close by her shoulder and sat solemnly up front. Leo sat beside his daughter and held her hand. Elyse, in a somber kaftan, was right by his side. But the kids—Susan and Roger—sat as far as possible from their estranged "sister," and Amanda realized those relationships would need a lot of work before the family approached normalcy.

The handful of attendees in the middle rows were likely Lynette's employed maids, perhaps a few neighbors. But generally it was a small sad group that paid little attention to the minister's generic service. Instead, they gazed out to sea, lost in their own thoughts.

Amanda imagined that by this evening, when Jo and Aqua gave them a farewell party at their restaurant, Lynette would be all but forgotten. Or she might think that by tomorrow night, when she and Sara were home in their respective towns of Mooresville and Charlotte, the whole experience would fade. But she would be wrong.

When the minister invited the family members to the edge of the ocean to scatter Lynette's ashes to the immortal deep, Amanda's gaze shifted to a large, powerful boat curving in, then out, at great speed—as though the captain was buzzing the shore.

"It's Troudeaux's cigarette boat!" Sara was astonished.

"Are you sure?" But then she recognized the sleek blue-and-gray hull. "He's gotta lotta nerve!" she hissed.

"Yes, but he's the one who got away. We'll never know his story." Sara quietly took her hand and squeezed hard. "And I don't want *you* to get away, Mandy." She paused as little Roger upturned the urn and spun out the last of the ashes.

A faraway look entered Sara's eyes as she peered out to sea. "Just because we have to go home, doesn't mean we can't be together. Will you come back here with me again next year?"

She gazed out at the powerful ocean, ever threatening to drag the very sands of the Outer Banks into oblivion. Then she remembered the strong beam of Hatteras Light, offering guidance and strength to all souls lost at sea. Finally, she looked back into the abiding light of Sara's foam-green eyes. "I will absolutely come," she whispered.

Bella Books, Inc.

*Women. Books. Even Better Together.*

P.O. Box 10543
Tallahassee, FL 32302

Phone: 800-729-4992
**www.bellabooks.com**